THE PECOS TRAIL

THE PECOS TRAIL

BRADFORD SCOTT

WHEELER
CHIVERS

This Large Print edition is published by Wheeler Publishing, Waterville, Maine, USA and by BBC Audiobooks Ltd, Bath, England.
Wheeler Publishing, a part of Gale, Cengage Learning.

The text of this Large Print edition is unabridged.
Other aspects of the book may vary from the original edition.
Set in 16 pt. Plantin.
Printed on permanent paper.

LIBRARY OF CONGRESS CATALOGING-IN-PUBLICATION DATA

Scott, Bradford, 1893–1975.
   The Pecos Trail / by Bradford Scott.
     p. cm. — (Wheeler Publishing large print western)
   ISBN-13: 978-1-59722-908-1 (pbk. : alk. paper)
   ISBN-10: 1-59722-908-3 (pbk. : alk. paper)
   1. Texas Rangers—Fiction. 2. Texas—Fiction. 3. Large type
books. I. Title.
PS3537.C9265P43 2009
813'.52—dc22
                                 2008045593

BRITISH LIBRARY CATALOGUING-IN-PUBLICATION DATA AVAILABLE

Published in 2009 in the U.S. by arrangement with Golden West Literary Agency.
Published in 2009 in the U.K. by arrangement with Golden West Literary Agency.

U.K. Hardcover: 978 1 408 43270 9 (Chivers Large Print)
U.K. Softcover: 978 1 408 43271 6 (Camden Large Print)

THE PECOS TRAIL

ONE

"Well, Shadow, there it is, the deadline for sheriffs! Was given that name quite a while back, and has lived up to it ever since. A deadline for Rangers? Well, horse, we'll see about that."

Sitting his magnificent black horse on the crest of a tall hill, Ranger Walt Slade gazed at the broad and turbulent stream winding and shining in the sun.

The Pecos is a long river, a strange and sinister river, a thousand miles of twisting canyon from the pine-clad mountains of New Mexico to the gray, bleak bluffs of the Rio Grande on the Texas border. Here is cattle country. Here will always be cattle country. The mountain brakes, the alkali flalts, the vast stretches of shifting sands, the treeless plains rolling to hills dim and distant on the skyline — these have never known and never will know the plough, save for narrow irrigated strips that are but nigh

7

invisible hairlines etching the stark immensities of the wastelands.

Trails cross the Pecos. Trails lurid in legend, grim in history. Where men bulk big and their exploits are stranger than any page dared by fiction. The Butterfield Trail, the Chihuahua, the San Antonio-El Paso. These are famous routes, by which the treasure of Mexico and the far West came east. There is, too, the waterless Goodnight-Loving Trail. And there are others.

Less known and less talked about, but surpassed by none in its saga of blood and violence, is the Pecos Trail. Less spoken of, too, is its crossing; but neither the Horsehead, Fort Lancaster, nor the Pontoon has a history of grim tragedy and despair to outshudder that of Bleached Bones Crossing, where the bluffs are the color of caked blood, and shadows stain the waters of the Pecos gloomy purple.

Bleached Bones got its name from the many skeletons that were, and still are, found half buried in the sands and the rusty clay.

And it was toward sinister Bleached Bones Crossing that Walt Slade gazed.

"Yes, there it is," Slade repeated. "And the trail down in that hollow must be the Pecos that will take us to Benton, the

8

railroad construction town we're headed for.

"That is if we can make it down this darned snake track without breaking both our necks," he added doubtfully.

Shadow snorted cheerfully as much as to say that he'd see to it that there weren't any broken necks. Slade chuckled, and studied the trail, little more than a game track, which slithered down over a series of benches, thickly grown with chaparral, that had the appearance of a gigantic and broken stair.

Walt Slade made a striking picture as he lounged easily atop his great horse with the grace of a lifetime in the saddle. He was very tall, more than six feet, and the breadth of his shoulders and the depth of his chest matched his height. The hair that showed beneath his battered, broad-brimmed "J.B." was so black that a blue shadow seemed to lie upon it. His eyes were clear gray — cold, reckless eyes with still a dancing light of laughter in their depths, rather long, thickly fringed with black lashes.

Those pale, watchful eyes, taken with the high-bridged nose and the grim lines of the long, powerful jaw and chin beneath a rather wide, humorous mouth, justified the name the *peons* of the Rio Grande River

9

villages had given Walt Slade *El Halcon,* The Hawk.

Slade wore the simple, efficient garb of the rangeland — faded blue overalls and equally faded soft blue shirt, open at the collar to reveal a bronzed, sinewy neck about which was looped a vivid handkerchief, batwing chaps, scuffed high-heeled half-boots of softly tanned leather. About his lean waist were double cartridge belts and from their carefully worked and oiled cut-out holsters protruded the plain black butts of heavy guns. A Winchester rifle snugged in the saddle boot beneath his muscular left thigh.

About to gather up the reins preparatory to urging Shadow forward, Slade suddenly relaxed again, his gaze fixed on a bend in the Pecos Trail on the far side of the river, about three miles distant. Around that bend had bulged a multitude of bouncing blobs over which hung a sun-shimmered cloud of dust.

"Trail herd headed this way," he remarked to Shadow. "A big one, too. Guess it's headed for Benton. We're in luck, horse. They can hardly reach the town before dark and are likely to bed down somewhere till morning. Means a surrounding of chuck and coffee for me, and a helping of oats for

10

you. We can use 'em; pouches have been empty since yesterday and I'm feeling a bit lank. I can't subsist on vegetation like you can, you old grass burner. Let's go. We should make it down to the Crossing before they get there. May be interesting to watch them hit the water, river high as it is. Let's go!"

From his high perch on the driver's seat of the chuck wagon, old man Trout looked over the sea of shaggy backs and tossing, gleaming horns. There was pride and satisfaction in the faded blue eyes of the Lazy K owner as he surveyed his great shipping herd rolling eastward under its cloud of dust; but there was anxiety, too. That herd was just about the Lazy K, so far as Trout hoping to hang onto the spread was concerned, and less than three miles ahead were two rows of ominous red bluffs breaking the rolling bronze-green of the rangeland.

Austere and menacing were those bluffs, devoid of vegetation for the most part, scored by washes, looming darkly against the clear blue of the Texas sky. Their rugged battlements seemed to voice a wordless threat. Their very silence implied a crouching monster waiting with infinite patience for a victim to come within reach. The

11

washes scoring them were as raw and ragged wounds gashed in the sides and flanks of the monster by gigantic claws.

And between those glowering bluffs flowed the murky, bitter waters of the Pecos.

As the herd began climbing the long slope which led to the barren crests of the hithermost bluffs, old man Trout's range boss, Ed Block, slowed down alongside the wagon.

"Another mile and we'll see what she looks like," he remarked. "That feller we met up the trail said she was high, but he got across, and I reckon we should, too."

"Different from a feller riding a good horse — a coupla thousand longhorns and a wagon," grunted Trout.

"Sure," agreed Block, "but we've made crossings in high water before."

"Uh-huh," Trout answered, adding pessimistically, "I hope we make this one. If we don't, the Lazy K is a goner, so far as we're concerned."

"What's eating you, John?" complained Block, with the familiarity of long service. "I've never seen you down in the dumps like this. Sure we'll make it."

"I hope so," Trout repeated. "Reckon it's because I've had to put up with so much bad luck the past year, Ed. It kinda gets a feller after a while. Right now, and you know

12

it, I'm pretty nigh to the end of my rope, and I'm depending on this herd getting through safe; everything's depending on it."

"Ain't nothing over bad to getting to the end of your rope so long as you're tied hard and fast," Block remarked wisely. "Buck up, Boss, you'll be swallerforkin' all over seven counties before the last brand's run. Those railroad construction fellers made us a mighty nice offer for this beef — better than the regular market price. We ain't licked yet, and I don't figure we're going to be."

"Hope not," Trout replied. "Well, here's the top of the sag. How does she look to you, Ed?"

Block gazed down the long slope before them to the dark waters worrying the reddish banks, and his eyes were thoughtful.

"She's high, all right," he admitted. "A hundred and fifty yards of swimming, I figure; that ain't over bad. I believe the boys can handle them through that; they've handled worse before now. How you going to manage it?"

Old John ran a calculating eye across the stream, hesitated, appeared to make up his mind.

"We'll shove the wagon in first," he decided. "The wagon is bound to drift down the stream a mite. I'll let her slide easy for a

13

while and then slant up stream. Let the beefs drink and then shove 'em in. Send them as straight across as you can. That way we should hit the far bank about the same time. Here we go!" He cracked his whip and the wagon rumbled down the slope toward the river's edge.

The wagon had been prepared for the crossing. To both sides had been attached long legs projecting beyond the ends. These would float the wagon and steady it. The vehicle had been carefully packed and everything lashed tight, so that there would be no shifting of the load to throw it off even keel.

John Trout was famous for his teamster skill. Rangy Weston, a young cowboy who was an expert swimmer, grasped the bridle reins of the near leader and led the team into the water. For a short distance the horses staggered and slipped as the river boiled about them. Another instant and they were swept off their feet. They sank until only their heads and shoulders showed above the surface, then struck out on the long swim across the swollen Pecos.

As Trout predicted, the wagon was washed down stream. He estimated the distance to cover, waited a mite more, then pointed his horses at an upstream angle.

At the same time, Ed Block and his rannies sent the cattle into the river with a rush. One moment the dark surface of the Pecos was unruffled save for the crests of foam here and there and the ominous bulk of a floating log or branch. The next it was crowded with shaggy backs, glinting horns, wildly rolling eyes.

Once started, the cows streaked it for the other side, bumping into tangled masses, filling the air with mad bawlings and the hollow clashing of horns. Everything seemed to be going ace-high.

Then abruptly the wagon got into trouble. The righthand swinger — one of the two horses in the middle of the six-horse team — caught its foreleg in the cross-tree of the leader ahead. It floundered, was thrown off its swimming stride. Under it went, and came up snorting and plunging.

Its terror was infectious. Its team-mates began cutting capers. Their antics set the loaded wagon to reeling and rocking and momentarily threatened an upset. Roaring threats and profanity, old John sent the whip lash snapping and snarling over the frantic swinger's back. With that threat directly above him, the swinger decided to swim, with only three legs if necessary. Rangy Weston fired off soothing yells to the lead-

15

ers. The wagon steadied, began making progress again. The far bank loomed closer. The herd was making good headway and was not in difficulty. Old John drew a deep breath of relief.

Then abruptly he let out a startled yelp. Rangy Weston swore a crackling oath. Farther up the stream, Ed Block yelled a futile warning to his hands, who were swimming their horses across and had little time for anything else. His yell was echoed by the spiteful crack of a rifle and a scream of despairing agony.

Two

Slade had reached the next to the bottom-most of the series of benches down which the track he was following wound. All the way he had ridden between stands of tall growth that rendered him invisible to anybody on the river bank. Now, however, he had a clear view of the trail coming up from the river and its environs. The bench on which he sat his horse was perhaps two score yards above the lowest, which flanked the trail, with a sharp slope littered with boulders and occasional straggles of growth tumbling down to the last bench and the trail.

The lowest bench, close to the shelving margin of the stream, was but a few yards above high water mark. It was dotted with thickets that flanked the crossing. Below the crossing the growth was unusually heavy, broken only by peculiar upward juts of stone, around which the flat surface of the bench coiled irregularly like a broken-backed snake.

From the elevation of the second bench, Slade had watched the Lazy K herd take the stream. He had noted with appreciaton John Trout's masterly handling of the bedeviled wagon team and had run an approving eye over the sleek beefs that breasted the turgid flood of the Pecos. Lounging in the saddle at the edge of the cleared space north of the crossing, he watched the progress of the herd.

Abruptly his glance fell to the lower bench and centered on the thicket which flanked the crossing; his keen eyes had noted movement there. The concentration furrow between his black brows deepened slightly as six men suddenly rode out of the thicket to face the river. All carried rifles and as they cleared the thicket they let the bridles fall onto the necks of their mounts.

Now, what the devil, El Halcon wondered.

The leaders of the swimming herd had just passed the middle of the stream. A young cowboy, his hat hanging on his shoulder by the chin strap, the sunlight gleaming golden on his curly yellow hair, was the foremost point man, holding some little distance back of the leaders. What happened next was so unexpected it caught

18

even El Halcon unprepared. One of the group that had emerged from the thicket threw his rifle to his shoulder. There was a wisp of smoke from the muzzle, the smashing crackle of the report.

The young point rider whirled from his saddle as if clutched by a mighty hand. He screamed once, a high-pitched cry of pain and terror, as his clawing fingers missed the trailing bridle. Then he vanished beneath the tossing waters, reappeared, swirling down stream, turning over and over, his helpless hands reaching out futilely. For an instant a curling ripple was stained with a froth of red.

The tight group by the river's edge let loose a storm of fire. Bullets flecked the water about the approaching cowboys. A hat was whirled from the head of one. Slade saw another duck frantically as whistling lead fanned his face. The cattle bawled with fright and began to mill.

Walt Slade went into action. With a flicker of movement he whisked his heavy Winchester from the boot. His gray eyes, now the color of frosted steel, glanced along the sights.

The rifle wisped smoke, bucked in his grasp. One of the drygulchers on the lower bench pitched from his saddle. The rifle spoke again and another man whirled downward to the red clay and lay shapeless as a sack of old clothes.

The four remaining owlhoots spun in their saddles with yells and curses and fired a volley at the dimly seen figure on the upper bench. Lead stormed about Slade. A bullet twitched his sleeve like an urgent hand. A second burned a red streak along one bronzed cheek. Then the Winchester spoke a third time. A yell from the lower bench echoed the report. A man dropped his rifle and clutched at his blood spouting shoulder.

One of the drygulchers bawled an order. He whirled his big bay and fled madly for the shelter of the growth on the far side of the trail, his three companions thundering behind him. Slade sent three more bullets whining after them and thought he saw a man sway in the hull, but could not be sure as the murderous quartet vanished into the brush.

Another flicker of movement and the Winchester was back in the boot. Slade's voice rang out like the peal of a great golden bell, "Trail, Shadow, trail!"

Instantly the great black horse shot downward across the slope that led to the lowest bench, slanting downstream in obedience to the pressure of El Halcon's knee. He dodged boulders or leaped over them, weaved around patches of growth, skittered, floundered, caught his balance and arrived at the lowest bench in a cloud of dust and a shower of stones. Over the lip he went and to the narrow stretch of broken beach where the water lapped. Slade sent him downstream at a racing run.

Slade let Shadow choose his own path. His eyes were fixed on the blob of gold that was the wounded cowboy's head. It vanished, reappeared. Slade caught a glimpse of feebly moving hands. The puncher was not dead and was trying to help himself with swiftly ebbing strength.

The flying horse passed the drowning man, raced onward for several hundred yards. Then Slade swerved him sharply to the right. Shadow took the water in a welter of foam and a cloud of sun-jewelled spray. A dozen floundering steps and he was swimming, breasting the current with iron muscles. Slade kept his head up, talked to him in cool, quiet tones, encouraged and steadied him with voice and hand. He dared not slip from the saddle and swim with the horse, for he would never be able to mount again with the half-drowned cowboy in his arms. And all the while his eyes were fixed on the floating body of the stricken point rider.

"It's going to be touch and go," he told the black horse as the angle between them and the man rapidly sharpened. "If he gets past he's a goner. No catching up with him in this current. Sift sand, jughead, or we've gotten wet for nothing."

The big horse snorted prodigiously, blew water from his flaring nostrils, rolled his effort-reddened eyes. He craned his neck, strained his great muscles to the utmost.

Downstream swept the wounded man. Slade noted that his hands no longer moved. Now he was almost abreast of the straining horse. Another dozen yards, a final mighty effort on Shadow's part. Slade leaned far over, flung out a long arm, clutched frantically through the spray and foam. The body swept past and Slade's steely fingers closed on a shirt collar.

Easily, as if the drowning man were a child, he lifted him from the water and cradled him in his arms. Shadow's head went under with the suddenly added weight, but almost instantly he broke surface, snorting equine profanity and, obedient to Slade's knee pressure, circled about, breasted the current and made for the shore.

But even his iron muscles were tiring. His

eyes were gorged with blood, he breathed in gurgling gasps. The added burden was telling on him.

His head went under again, and again he fought his way back to the surface. He showed no signs of panic. There was no hint of fear in his great, liquid, intelligent eyes. The current swept him downstream despite his struggles.

"Looks like we're going to take the Big Jump together," his grim-faced rider muttered.

Then suddenly horse and rider swirled sideways in an eddy. The current gripped them harder than ever, but now it hurled them straight toward the benched bluffs they had quitted. Another moment of exhausting struggle and Shadow's irons clashed on the rocky bottom. He reeled and staggered through the shoaling water and halted on the shelving bank, head hanging, front legs spread wide.

Slade slipped to the ground, still gripping his unconscious burden. He stroked the horse's nose with his free hand.

"Thanks, feller," he said simply.

But Shadow seemed to understand.

El Halcon placed the unconscious cowboy on the ground, swiftly cut away the right shoulder of his shirt and examined the

23

wound. It was high up through the shoulder and had bled profusely. He straightened up, strode to where Shadow still stood with hanging head and from his saddle pouch took a small pot of antiseptic ointment and a roll of bandage, well soaked but otherwise in good condition. Working deftly and swiftly, he padded and strapped the wound. He straightened up again with a nod of satisfaction.

The herd was rolling up the trail that led from the crossing. The chuck wagon had just made the bank. A horseman raced along the bank to where Slade stood. It was Ed Block, the Lazy K range boss. He flung himself from his dripping saddle beside Slade.

"The kid bad hurt?" he asked anxiously.

"Nothing to worry about," Slade told him. "Lost considerable blood and swallowed a bit of water, but he'll be coming out of it in a jiffy. See, his eyelids are already fluttering. Should be able to handle his chores in a month or so, I'd say. Anybody else catch it? No? That's good. Looked bad for a few minutes, but everything turned out okay, I guess."

He smiled down at Block from his great height, his even teeth flashing startlingly white in his bronzed face.

The grizzled old range boss stuck out his hand. "Block's my name, feller, Ed Block," he said in a voice that quivered with emotion. "I'm range boss for the Lazy K outfit, and I want to thank you for all of us for what you did, before the rest of the boys get here and thank you for themselves."

El Halcon gripped the gnarled old hand in his slim fingers and supplied his own name. "Real glad to know you, Block," he said.

Old Ed gazed at the Hawk's towering form with frank admiration, and paid him the highest compliment rangeland has to offer.

"Slade," he said, "I've known a heap of prime men in my time, but I never clapped eyes on one I'd rather ride the river with than you!"

THREE

John Trout and the rest of the outfit arrived a few minutes later and were profuse in their thanks. They carried the wounded cowboy, who had regained consciousness and was puffing on a cigarette, to the chuck wagon and made him comfortable.

"Reckon we'd better make camp up on top of the sag and bed the critters down," Block decided. "We can't make it to town before dark and I figure everybody's about fagged anyhow. We'd have been a heap worse fagged if it hadn't been for Slade, and the herd would have gone to glory."

"To Mexico, more likely," said Trout. "After they'd finished us all off, those hellions would have had clear going to the Border."

Slade was gazing speculatively at the flooded Pecos, the concentration furrow deep between his black brows, a sure sign El Halcon was doing some hard thinking.

But he only nodded in reply to Trout's words and offered no comment.

"Before you roll on, there's a chore I want to attend to," he said. "I'd like for you to come along with me, sir, if you don't mind."

"Certainly," replied the Lazy K owner. "Ed, you get the cows moving up the sag. I'll follow with the wagon as soon as I'm finished with what Slade wants. What is it, son?"

Slade abruptly added to his original request. "Bring your whole outfit along for a few minutes," he said.

Trout glanced at him wonderingly but relayed the request in the form of an order. Slade led the way to where the bodies of the two slain drygulchers lay huddled at the edge of the thicket.

"Look them over, all of you, and see if you can recognize either of them," he directed.

The cowboys peered at the contorted faces and shook their heads.

"Ornery looking specimens," one observed, "but I don't remember ever clapping eyes on either of them before. There are their horses standing up the trail a-piece. Mexican skillet-of-snakes brands but good looking critters and good rigs. I wouldn't mind having the sorrel for my string, if it's

27

okay with everybody."

"And I sorta favor the roan," said Rangy Weston, "that is, if nobody objects."

Slade offered no comment, although he had learned from observation that taking over owlhoot stock was not always a good thing. He nodded to Trout.

"Get the cows moving, boys," said the owner. "All finished, Slade?"

"Not quite," El Halcon replied. "You stay with me a mite longer, if you don't mind. I'm going to give those carcasses a once-over, and I'd like for you to check what I find."

He squatted beside the bodies and turned out their pockets, revealing a surprisingly large amount of money in gold and silver.

"Hellions been doing themselves proud," growled Trout. "They never got that much dinero working for forty-per."

"Take it and divide it among your boys," Slade suggested. "I figure they've earned it. Leave it on them and the sheriff will shove it in the county treasury, which I imagine can do without it."

"Guess it can, anyhow it's going to," chuckled Trout as he pocketed the coin. "Find anything else?"

"Nothing of any value so far," Slade answered. "Hello, what's this?"

From an inner pocket he had drawn a folded sheet of paper. He unfolded it and glanced at the cryptic lines and figures traced on it in a neat hand. His brows drew together and his eyes darkened with thought. He passed Trout the paper without comment.

The Lazy K owner took it and studied it, turned it sideways, then upside down, and shook his head.

"I can't make no sense of it," he admitted. "Looks like a lot of doo-dads the hellion was drawing to kill time."

He passed the paper back to Slade, who refolded it and slipped it in his pocket.

"Keep it for a souvenir," he explained.

"I once knew a feller who'd always cut off the trigger fingers of jiggers he cashed in, smoke 'em and carry 'em in his pockets," Trout remarked reminiscently.

"Everybody to their taste, as the old lady said when she kissed the cow," Slade smiled. "Well, I guess there's nothing more we can do except notify the sheriff of what happened."

"There's a deputy stationed at Benton," Trout said. "He can come down and look the carcasses over if he wants to waste the time. I'll get that wagon rolling so the boys

29

can eat as soon as they finish bedding down."

Slade retrieved Shadow, who appeared to have suffered no ill effects from his exhausting experience. Trout climbed to the seat beside the cook, who had remained with the wagon, and followed the drag up the slope. Slade lingered a moment for a last look at the faces of the dead outlaws.

The face of the bulky man from whose pocket he had taken the paper was not a pleasant face, but Slade conceded it was an able one, although contradictory as to feature, with the brow of a thiner and a well shaped nose. But the glazed eyes were small and piggish, set deep in rolls of fat, and despite the powerful lines of the long jaw, the mouth and chin were weak, which the short, slightly grizzled beard and mustache could not quite conceal.

Been somebody once, but couldn't hold his stirrups, Slade concluded. Got pitched and took up with the wrong crowd and finished with his boots on.

He examined the dead man's hands. They were well shaped and powerful, well cared for, with clean nails. The palms were firm but devoid of callouses. Not the hands of one accustomed to hard physical work.

The second outlaw was scrawny and

30

emaciated. He had tufted brows, a crooked nose and a cruel mouth gashing his cadaverous face like a raw knife cut. Queer looking callouses on his thumbs and forefingers hinted at the quick-draw man with both hands. Slade spared him but a passing glance before he mounted Shadow and rode after the wagon.

"Well, horse, we've made a start," he remarked. "When Captain Jim headed us this way, he said this section needed cleaning up. Looks like he was right, per usual. But horse, what I'd like to know is what's the meaning of what happened today. Trout and Block and the rest of the Lazy K outfit set it down as just a regulation widelooping try; but it wasn't. If those hellions had killed the Lazy K hands, as they showed every indication of trying to do, the herd would have milled in the middle of the river and been swept away. Not a hoof would have reached the east bank. Those devils must have known that. In other words, they didn't want the cows to make land; their plan was to send them down the flooded river to drown. Just a couple of miles to the south is a sheer-walled canyon with the water lapping the stone. The general idea appears to have been the destruction of forty thousand dollars' worth of cattle and, presumably,

31

mass murder. And to top things off, a drygulcher is packing an extremely well done plat of a cadastral and topographical survey in his pocket. What would a hellion of his apparent calibre be doing with a thing like that? What the devil *have* we stumbled into? Well, as I've told you before, time that grinds the rocks will tell us all. So heads up, horse, and let's go! Anyhow, it looks like we are in for an interesting time of it."

The Lazy K made a comfortable camp atop the bluffs, from where there was a good view in every direction. Ed Block took no chances, however, and doubled the force of night hawks who kept guard over the cows through the hours of darkness.

Shortly after daybreak the herd rolled on. It did not graze along slowly in a great arrowhead formation, point to the front, but in a long snaky line, for Block was determined to cover the twelve miles of distance to Benton by late afternoon and pushed the cows.

"No more night camps if I can help it," he told Slade. "May run a few pounds of fat off them this way, but the quicker they're safe in the railroad corral the better I'll feel. What happened yesterday shook me a bit and I don't want another such experience."

About three miles of trail had been covered when Slade saw, beyond a belt of tall chaparral, smoke rising against the sky.

"The railroad," said Block. "They're building fast as they can. Slanting south, now, to where they'll cross the Pecos three miles or so down-river. The bridge across the river is already up. That old rannie they call Jaggers Dunn, who runs the C. & P., is quite a feller. Shoved in all the materials needed for the bridge by way of twenty-mule-team wagons. Folks said it couldn't be done, but he did it."

Slade, who counted General Manager James G. "Jaggers" Dunn as one of his closest friends, smiled slightly.

"Ten miles to the south another railroad is building west, the M. K. Understand the two roads ain't over friendly to each other," observed Block.

Slade knew that another epochal railroad race for El Paso, "the Pass of the North," where the coast-to-coast rails would cross the Rocky Mountains, was under way. The loser would not only forfeit valuable mail and express contracts but would have to enter into an agreement with the winner to use the latter's trackage for the more than eighty miles west from Sierra Blanca to El Paso. Both lines were straining every nerve to lay steel in the Pass first. And they still

33

had a long ways to go, with the Pecos Crossing one of the more important focal points. Precious miles would be gained by the road that first made the crossing and the difficult terrain to the west of the river.

A little later the riders passed through the chaparral belt and a scene of intense activity unfolded before their eyes. Far into the east, until they seemed to draw together, stretched twin ribbons of steel shimmering in the sunlight. At the west end of the railhead, men wielded shovels and picks and ponderous sledges. To Slade's ears came the rhythmic clink of mauls on spike-heads as brawny hammer-men spiked the rails to the crossties. Far in advance were the graders, picking and shovelling and levelling. A locomotive chugged slowly forward on the new-laid steel, shoving a long line of gondolas and flat cars ahead of it. From the gondolas laborers tossed creosoted crossties that others laid in place on the completed grade. From the flat cars steel rails were levered clanging to the ground and were gripped with tongs by the steelmen who staggered along with the ponderous thirty-foot lengths to place them on the ties. Spurs paralleled the main lines and on these other locomotives moved material trains. Smoke streaked with steam spouted from the stacks of the chug-grumbling engines. The hammer of the exhausts blended with the grind of the great drivers, the raffle and clang of brake rigging, the pound of colliding couplings and the continuous musical crash of steel on steel.

As they drew nearer, their nostrils were stung by the reek of coal smoke, the raw tang of creosote, the pungent odor of hot oil and the fragrance of newly turned earth. The swinging spike mauls were circles of flaming light. The newly laid steel glowed redly under the sun. The purplish gray of the creosoted ties smoldered dully. The red and blue shirts of the workers moved in a kaleidoscope against the background of the green grass and chaparral and the yellow earth. The voices of foremen could be heard shouting orders, while the hammer wielders raised a melodious chant in time to the beat and swing of their mauls. The shovels of the gandy-dancers clinked and clattered as the workers stamped earth and stone beneath the ties, their feet rising and falling in the queer shuffle that gave them their name.

Far to the east a whistle wailed thinly. A black streak was boring westward toward the railhead.

"That's a work train bringing more men," Block observed. "They're sure shoving this road along; but they'll slow up when they get past the Pecos; bad country over there."

The toilers paused to wave their hats and cheer lustily as the herd streamed past.

"There go our beefsteaks!" one bellowed. "Drill, ye terriers, drill! Meat on the table tonight!"

A little later the work train thundered past with booming exhaust, clanging siderods and spinning drive wheels. The workers packing the cars also cheered and waved. The cowboys waved back as the train roared onward and swirling clouds of smoke almost hid riders and cattle.

"Whew!" coughed Block. "Railroads are okay and we need 'em, but they sure make for hard breathing."

A few minutes more, however, and they were out of the smoke reek and again inhaling the clean air of the rangeland.

And far ahead a dark smudge fouled the clean blue of the Texas sky, rising almost to the zenith, glinting in the sunlight, changing shape under the kneading fingers of the wind.

"And that," said Ed Block, "is Benton. That's the smoke from the shops and roundhouses."

John Trout was yelping something from the chuck wagon. Slade and Block pulled

36

up to catch what he was saying.

"Come sit with me a while, son," he called to Slade. "I want to talk to you. One of the boys can lead your cayuse."

"Guess he won't need leading," Slade replied cheerfully as he knotted the split reins, dropped them on Shadow's neck and swung up to the high seat. "Follow, Shadow!"

The big black obediently took up a position behind the wagon. Old John swore with admiration.

"Darned if I don't believe that horse understands everything you say to him," he declared.

"I guess he comes pretty close to it," Slade conceded. "You wish to speak to me about something, sir?"

"Yep, I do," said Trout. "As it happens I'm a mite shorthanded right now, and Chuck getting drilled through the shoulder and laid up for a spell doesn't help. How about signing on with me? Tophand wages and a little better."

"Thank you, sir, for the offer," Slade replied. "I'll think on it. I'll help with this shipping herd chore and maybe ride back to your spread with you, but I'd like a few days just to take it easy and look around a bit. Then perhaps I'll take you up on it."

37

"Okay, we'll let it ride at that," said Trout. "If you decide to sign on, your pay starts from yesterday. Hope you will."

The sun was well down the western sky when the tired and dusty cattle finally rolled into Benton and headed for the railroad construction stock yard. Slade gazed around him with interest.

In the midst of the rolling prairie, Benton lay in sprawled ugliness. Shacks, dobes, even tents supplied shelter for the railroad workers. Long lines of camp cars on sidings supplemented the more permanent abodes. The main street of the town was lined with garish false-fronts, flimsy and rawly new.

Slade had gathered from Block that Benton was to be a General Division point for the C. & P. and a junction for the line later to be built south into Mexico. But glancing about with an experienced eye, Slade doubted it. The layout was certainly not elaborate enough. There was a small roundhouse, a machine shop and a considerable web of track, but nothing to what he felt was to be expected. Interesting, he thought.

The tedious chore of the weighing-in promised to consume the rest of the afternoon. There were more than enough Lazy K cowboys to handle the chore, Block told Slade.

"No sense in you hanging around," he said. "Put your cayuse in the railroad barn — he'll be well taken care of — and have a look-see at the town. The Queen High saloon is about the best for a drink and something to eat. Feller named Richmond Hurst runs it, and he's quite a feller. Salty as they come. This is a rough pueblo, but Hurst knows how to handle 'em and foolin' with him sure ain't healthy. Funny about him. He's setting up a place in Muerto, the cowtown six miles to the south of our ranchhouse. A great big place plumb well built, and I saw some of the furnishings going in. Plumb out of line for a town like Muerto which never has amounted to much and never will. Maybe he knows what he's doing, though. Always seems to. John and me will meet you at the Queen High and we'll eat together. Okay?"

Slade promised to be there. He stabled his horse and sauntered along the main street. With the construction workers mostly on the job, the street was comparatively quiet, but Slade suspected that it would be far from quiet in a couple of hours, after the work trains boomed in and the railroaders went looking for diversion.

Slade had walked some little distance down the street when he approached a rather more substantial looking building which boasted a sign that read, "Queen High." Evidently the place Block had mentioned as run by one Richmond Hurst. He was directly opposite the plate glass window when a big, burly looking cowboy ran through the swinging door, banging them open with a force that threatened to take them off their hinges. Slade paused and stared in mild astonishment.

It was not the fact that the cowboy ran through the doors that surprised him, but the reason for his running. Close behind him, gripping him by the collar and the seat of his pants was an individual of singular and striking appearance. He was not over five feet tall but he was about as broad as he was long. He had bristling carroty hair, enormous handlebar mustaches and sad brown eyes like those of a spaniel dog.

The cowboy reached the edge of the board sidewalk, shot through the air as if he had taken unto himself wings and landed on his face in the dust of the street. His propellant stood batting his enormous hands together as if to free them from dust.

The cowboy rolled over, staggered to his feet and shook his fist at his adversary.

"Some day you'll do that once too often!"

he bellowed, and lurched off down the street.

The broad dwarf was still batting his hands, together. "He was droonk and dishorderly," he observed to Slade and waddled back into the saloon.

"Chucks Butch out on his ear that way about three times every week," a bystander explained to Slade.

Chuckling, Slade followed the dwarf through the swinging doors. Evidently the Queen High owner was all Block said he was.

The bar was fairly well occupied. Slade finally found a place at the far end, where stood a tall, slim but broad-shouldered elegant man, faultlessly garbed in funeral black relieved only by the snow of his ruffled shirt front. His face was dark, almost swarthy, and his meticulously groomed hair was black as Slade's own. In startling contrast to his complexion, his eyes were a very pale blue, the cold blue of a glacier lake. He ran their quick gaze over Slade's form and face and his teeth flashed white in a cordial smile as he made way for him at the bar.

"Have a drink," he invited, motioning to a nearby bartender.

"Thank you, guess I can stand one," Slade accepted. He glanced across the room

41

toward where the truculent dwarf was moving about, his brown eyes taking in everything.

"Reckon that sawed-off gent who just helped another gent out the door is Richmond Hurst, the owner?" he remarked interrogatively.

The other smilingly shook his head.

"No," he replied in a voice as musical as the vibration of a silver guitar string. "That is Algernon Ragnall, my floor manager. I am Richmond Hurst."

Four

Slade regarded the slender, broad-shouldered man with renewed interest. His slenderness, he decided, was that of a tempered sword blade. There was a steely quality about him and his movements were graceful and assured.

Hurst raised his glass with a slim, aristocratic-looking hand and nodded over the rim.

"New in this section?" he asked pleasantly as he replaced the empty glass on the bar.

"Got in about an hour back," Slade equivocated. Hurst nodded and gestured to the bartender to refill the glasses.

"Hope you'll decide to stay," he said. "We need new men of the right sort in this section. What the big open spaces of Texas need more than anything else is people of the right sort. That's what I'm hoping for most from the railroads. They should bring in home seekers, and folks with notions for developing the country. This is a potentially rich section. Its great drawback has been isolation. Farther to the south the road which went through some years back changed that whole terrain. Plenty of prime beef being raised here, but not nearly as much as the land can sustain. Gold and other minerals in the mountains. Wouldn't be surprised if oil and natural gas will sooner or later be struck in this region. But it takes people to bring all those things to pass. Everything is here and waiting. All that's needed is folks with ideas and the get-up to put them over. Excuse me a minute."

He walked with lithe strides to a nearby table where an argument over a poker hand was growing heated. He spoke to the players and Slade noted that as he did so his voice underwent a subtle change; it became harsh and deep.

The warning was effective. The poker players cooled down. Hurst strolled back to the bar. He looked Slade over with a speculative eye.

"Cowboy?" he stated rather than asked, glancing keenly at The Hawk's slender, sinewy hands.

Smiling slightly, Slade turned them palms up. "Nope, no rope or branding burns right now," he replied, reading the intent of the other's glance. "I was range boss for the last spread for which I worked." (Which was perfectly true.)

Hurst flushed slightly but did not raise his eyes. Slade knew that he was studying the callouses on thumb and forefinger — the callouses made by the curved, bevel-edge steel of a trigger and the milled tip of a gun hammer.

"Yes, I like to shoot, and I practice the draw considerably," Slade said softly.

Hurst jerked his head up. "You're too darned good at reading what's in the other fellow's mind," he remarked in exasperated tones and with startling frankness.

Then he smiled, a very charming smile, but one which, Slade thought, never quite reached his pale eyes.

"I have to try to get a line on the gents who drop into my place," he said. "No offense intended."

"None taken," Slade replied. "Well, we'll have another drink together and then I think I'll sit down at one of the tables and have a smoke and a cup of coffee. I promised a couple of friends I'd meet them here for something to eat."

Hurst nodded and gestured for a waiter to prepare a table. They finished their drinks

45

and Slade drew up a chair to the table and relaxed comfortably over his coffee and cigarette. The while he speculated about the saloonkeeper, who struck him as being an exception to his class. Hurst dressed like a gambler and looked a good deal like one; but he spoke in the terms of a businessman. Slade had not failed to remark his unusual mode of speech. It was cultured, but liberally spiced with rangeland expressions. He wondered if Richmond Hurst had two sides to him. Ed Block had hinted that Hurst was a salty individual with whom it was dangerous to tangle. Slade was of the opinion that Block had the right of it.

Slade finished a couple of cigarettes and a like number of cups of coffee. Trout and Block did not put in an appearance. Finally, growing restless, he rejoined Richmond Hurst at the end of the bar.

At that moment the swinging doors banged open and a small group of men in the rough garb of the railroad workers swaggered in and found places at the bar. They were big men and muscular and Slade noted that they wore guns and knives. They downed straight whiskey in gulps, talking loudly among themselves.

Several minutes passed, and suddenly Slade sensed a stiffening of Hurst's lean body. A second group of men, about equal in number to the railroad builders, had entered. They were also big men for the most part, wearing rangeland clothes, and all were armed. They shouldered their way to the bar near the first group and ordered drinks.

"There's the making of trouble here now," Hurst remarked in low tones.

He was right, and it did not take long to develop. Soon it was apparent that the two groups were tossing remarks at each other. Abruptly the bar exploded in hectic action. Fists thudded, men strained and wrestled. Chairs and tables were overturned, glasses smashed.

Algernon Ragnall, the floor manager, came bounding across the room, roaring with indignation, and hurled men right and left. Hurst also darted forward and bored his way between the combatants, who continued to shout and curse and swing wild blows. The uproar increased until the hanging lamps danced with the racket.

Then suddenly someone pulled a gun. A shot rang out, the bullet thudding into the ceiling. Hurst knocked the gunman backward with a driving blow straight from the shoulder, which was partly blocked. At the same instant steel flickered in another hand.

Walt Slade, who had been watching the rukus with mild and somewhat puzzled interest, streaked from the bar as an arc of flashing light drove straight for Hurst's back.

Before the blade reached its mark, slim fingers like rods of nickel steel closed on the knife wielder's wrist and halted it in mid-air. He yelled with agony as Slade's iron grip ground the bones of his wrist together. The knife tinkled to the floor, the man writhed about and struck a blow at Slade's face.

It had not traveled six inches when it was blocked. Slade whirled the man around, shifted his grip to his collar and the seat of his pants, jerked him off his feet, swung him forward and let go.

The big fellow shot through the air like a projectile. He took one of the swinging doors from its hinges and thudded to the board sidewalk. He did not come back. His companions turned on Slade, yelling curses.

Slade's hands flickered down and up. The two groups "froze," staring at the yawning black muzzles that seemed to single every man out for individual attention, and back of those rock-steady muzzles were the terrible eyes of El Halcon.

Slade spoke, his voice still quiet and musical, but the voice of the Texas Ranger who expects, and gets, obedience.

"That will be all," he said. "Outside, the lot of you, and it would be a good idea not to come back tonight."

There was a moment of hesitancy, shuffling feet. Then in the sudden silence the double click of the cocking hammers sounded plainly.

That ended the business. The men, sullen, glowering, headed for the door. Slade watched them pass out, holstered his guns and turned back to the bar. He raised a brimming glass with a hand that did not spill a drop. The shaking bartender gulped in his throat.

Richmond Hurst returned to the bar. He regarded Slade strangely for a moment. "Thanks," he said. "If it hadn't been for you, I'd have very likely gotten an airhole in my hide."

"Possibly," Slade conceded. "What was the row about?"

"It's happened before, though not as bad as tonight," Hurst replied. "There's trouble every now and then between the cowhands and the railroaders. Some of the oldtime owners hereabouts don't favor the roads coming through, say they just make trouble and disrupt the existing order of things. Which they do, to a certain extent. Naturally

49

their hands follow their line of thinking and now and then have a mixup with the construction men, especially after the whiskey gets to buzzing in their ears."

Slade nodded without comment. He wondered if Hurst really believed what he said. For Slade knew very well that the fight was staged and as phony as a seven-dollar bill. Presumably with the intent of getting Hurst embroiled and killing him under cover of the general row. A most unfortunate "accident!"

Hurst again looked Slade up and down. "I wouldn't have believed there was a man in Texas who could handle that big fellow as you did, throwing him clean through the door," he observed.

"Guess he was sort of headed that way, which made it easier," Slade smiled.

"Yes, he was headed that way, all right," Hurst agreed dryly. "His feet never touched the floor till he hit the sidewalk."

In the railroad office, old John Trout counted over the thick sheaf of big bills the purchasing agent handed him. He carefully stowed the packet in an inside pocket with a buttoned flap, said goodnight to the agent and left the office, Block walking beside him. Outside the door he paused, eyeing the sky, in which the first stars were appearing. Benton was beginning to roar. Work trains had been pulling into the yards for some time, each disgorging its load of toilers who soon would crowd the bars to capacity. Riders from the various neighboring spreads clattered along the main street, and there were also other riders with shadowy antecedents, dubious presents and highly problematical futures. Trout shook his gray head.

"Ed," he said, "I'm scairt. This is one devil of a lot of dinero to be packing around in a town like this after dark. I'm glad we've got that Slade feller with us, but just the same I'm bad worried. I wish this money was tucked away in the ranchhouse safe, or at the bank, paying off that infernal note."

"I know how you feel," Block nodded. "And I feel sort of the same way. Maybe I imagined it, but it seemed to me quite a few gents looked us over careful like this evening. And I keep thinking of what happened yesterday at the Crossing. Those hellions knew we were on the way here with the cows and were laying for us. And those that got away, and maybe some more belonging to the outfit, would know you'd get paid for the cows when they were delivered. And I can't forget how those three hellions

51

in the saloon right across the street looked us over when we dropped in for a sandwich and a cup of coffee. Ornery sidewinders or I never saw one. They looked as if they were expecting us and were glad to see us. Yep, I'm worried, too, with the boys scattered all over town and getting drunk."

"Let's hustle over to the Queen High and meet Slade," said Trout. "That young feller is one salty jigger, and don't you forget it. I'll feel better with him setting alongside me."

Block was silent a moment, then, "Boss," he said, "I've got a suggestion to make. Nobody but you and me knows that Slade has just about agreed to sign on with us. If he happened to slide out of town tonight, nobody would be apt to think anything of it. Suppose you send him to the ranch with the dinero. Have him ride tonight, right away. His horse is a sand sifter if there ever was one. Even if somebody did catch on, there wouldn't be a Chinaman's chance of them overtaking him."

Old John stared at his range boss. "But, Ed," he protested, "we hardly know that feller. Don't know anything about him, where he came from, or nothing. He was mighty vague when I asked him a question or two about himself — said he was just

52

passing through when he saw what was going on at the Crossing and figured he'd oughta take a hand. It'd be one devil of a chance to take with a feller who's a plumb stranger."

"Boss," Block replied, "you've took my judgment on men a lot of times before now. Did you ever know me to be wrong?"

"Nope, I never did," Trout admitted. "You seem to be able to size a feller up pronto, no matter what brand he seems to be wearing. Uh-huh, I've backed your judgment to the limit before now, and I've never had cause to regret it."

"Okay, then back it now," said Trout. "I'll go bail for that big feller. I tell you it's the plumb smart thing to do."

"All right, I'll chance it," Trout agreed reluctantly. "But if you're wrong this time, Ed, you'll mighty soon be looking for a job of riding for somebody else, because there won't be any hiring done by me. I'll be twirling a loop for somebody else like the rest of you, and I'm not exactly as young as I used to be. Okay, though, we'll meet Slade in the Queen High and tell him what's in the wind."

FIVE

Still standing at the bar with Hurst, Slade saw Trout and Block enter and glance around expectantly. He led them to the table that was waiting for them and they gave their orders to a waiter. Trout wasted no time outlining Block's suggestion. Slade regarded him curiously — Dunn drummed the desk top with his fingers a moment

"Don't you think you're taking a big chance with a stranger?" he asked.

"Yes, I am," Trout admitted frankly. "But Ed here says I'm not, and Ed is usually right about anything he says, so I'm taking it. Here — I'm slipping you the money under the table."

Slade took the thick packet and expertly stowed it away, confident that nobody had noted the transaction.

"I'll ride soon as I've finished eating," he said. "Did you get in touch with the deputy sheriff relative to what happened at the

Crossing?"

"He's out of town, won't be back till later," replied Trout. "That's another thing that had me bothered. We'll see him as soon as he comes in."

Slade nodded. "Now give me directions as to how to get to your ranchhouse from the Pecos Trail," he said.

Block proceeded to do so. "So you see you can't miss it," he concluded. "We'll see you there tomorrow."

Slade smiled down at the little foreman, and his eyes were abruptly sunny as summer seas.

"Yes, you'll see me there," he said. "But I want you two to be careful tonight. If I were you, I wouldn't stay out too late unless you can round up some of your boys to keep you company."

"That's a notion, all right," agreed Block. "Maybe we can grab onto some of the young hellions, if they ain't all too drunk or gallivantin' off somewhere with gals. We —" his voice abruptly trailed off Slade saw that he was staring at three men who had just entered the saloon.

"John," he said hoarsely, "them's the three devils who were looking us over so close this afternoon."

"Darned if you ain't right!" exclaimed

55

Trout. "They're looking around like they're hunting somebody."

"Forget them!" Slade snapped. "Don't let them know you've noticed them. Keep your eyes on the table; I'm watching them in the back bar mirror."

Trout and Block obeyed, giving their attention to the food the waiter had just brought.

"They've spotted us," Slade said quietly a moment later. "They're looking us over, all right." He buttered a piece of bread with great nicety, apparently absorbed in the chore at hand, but never losing sight of the unsavory trio who had found places at the bar and were muttering together One was tall, well set-up The lower portion of his face was covered with a thick black beard and his hatbrim was drawn low, so that little was to be seen of his features other than hair and a glint of eyes in the shadow of the hat. Slade's eyes were thoughtful as he noted the limpness of the beard.

Of the other two, one was medium as to height and build. He had a grubby face and there was nothing outstanding about him. The third man had a furtive, slinking gait and a rat face. He was slight and scrawny with narrow shoulders and a pigeon breast. The sort that evoluted from the snake rather than from the monkey, one would say.

Slade was pretty well convinced that he and his companions were the subject of the low-voiced conversation going on between the three and there was an amused gleam in his eyes. He smiled thinly when, a little later, the small man unobtrusively left the saloon. His companions remained at the bar, drinking and talking.

After finishing a final cup of coffee, Slade stood up. "See you tomorrow," he said, and sauntered toward the door. He knew the gaze of the two men at the bar was following him. At the door he turned, met their eyes squarely, smiled derisively and as the pair gaped in astonishment passed out into the night. Walking neither fast nor slow, he headed for the railroad stable where he had left Shadow. He got the rig on quickly, mounted and rode out of town. As soon as he reached the Pecos Trail his voice rang out —

"Trail, Shadow, trail!"

Instantly the big black lunged forward. In a moment he was going like the wind. Slade chuckled; he had not the slightest fear of pursuit.

In the Queen High, old John heaved a sigh of relief. "Somehow or other I feel a sight better," he said.

Block chucked "You'll feel still better tomorrow night," he predicted.

"Hope so," replied Trout. "Let's slide down to the Bear Cat for a drink. I left word at Deputy Sullivan's office that he'd find us there if we weren't in the Queen High. It's quieter, and some of the boys will be sure to drop in there later."

A few minutes after they left the saloon, the little rat-faced man entered and sidled up to his companions.

"It's going to be a cinch," he whispered. "The two old coots are at the Bear Cat by themselves. Their hands are scattered all over town, getting loaded. And that big ice-eyed hellion is gone — forked his horse and rode out of town."

The tall man jumped as if a scorpion had bit him. "What's that?" he exclaimed. "Gone? Which way did he go?"

"West along the Pecos Trail. 'Peared to be in a hurry. Why?"

The big man swore viciously, in low tones, and dropped his hand to the butt of his gun. "Snake," he rasped, "I've a notion to gut-shoot you and leave you to die sweating!"

The rat-faced man dodged back as if the other had launched a blow at him "Wh-what?" he quavered "Wh-what's the matter?"

58

"Matter!" raged the tall man in a hissing whisper. "Why, you terrapin-brained idiot, that big devil's got the money with him, that's what's the matter. No wonder he grinned at us when he walked out! They put it over on us proper, and you didn't have the sense to savvy what was going on. You let him ride away right under your nose with all that dinero. Wait till the Boss hears about this! You'll be lucky not to lose any more than your ears!"

The little man's face was ashen; his beady eyes darted about as if seeking some avenue of escape. "L-let's get after him, he ain't been gone long, we can catch him up before he makes the river," he stuttered.

The other ground his teeth in futile fury. "Catch him up, the devil!" he spat. "There isn't a bronk in Texas could catch up with that black horse with half an hour's start. We've got to move fast. The Boss must hear about this pronto, so he can make other plans."

He glanced toward the far end of the bar, where Richmond Hurst stood, seemed to hesitate, change his mind. "Come on," he said. "Let's get out of here."

"I — I don't want to go!" wailed Snake in a thin, high whisper.

"You're going," the other told him grimly.

59

"Maybe he'll give you a chance to square yourself — maybe. Say by doing away with that big ice-eyed hellion who put it over on us. You're good at that sort of thing, even if you haven't any brains. Come on!"

In the Bear Cat saloon, John Trout and Block were drinking leisurely at the bar and discussing future plans. As they stood in satisfied appreciation of good liquor, a lanky, gray-faced individual entered, nodded to them and stood looking over the crowd with keen, searching eyes, as if seeking a familiar face. They recognized the newcomer as Mark Sullivan, Sheriff Ad Dobson's chief deputy, who was stationed at the turbulent construction town.

Apparently unsuccessful in his quest for somebody he expected, perhaps hoped to find at the Bear Cat, Sullivan sauntered to the bar and joined the two cattlemen. He accepted an invitation to have a drink and surveyed old John over the rim of his glass.

"Hear you're taking up with prime company of late, John," he observed.

Trout looked puzzled. "What you getting at, Mark?" he asked.

"Oh, nothing much, just heard you rode in with El Halcon this afternoon. Several folks recognized him."

"El Halcon!"

"Uh-huh. Heard tell of him, eh?"

"Who the devil hasn't?" growled Trout. "What you talking about, Mark? I haven't seen El Halcon."

"Eyesight must be getting pretty bad in your old age, John," the deputy replied "Can't see past your bridle hand, eh? Big tall feller, black hair, gray eyes, hawk nose. Packs two guns. Rides a black horse the kind that ain't seen often. Oh, you did see him, then?"

Old John was staring at the deputy, his eyes nearly popping from his head, his jaw sagging.

"S-Slade?" he gasped. "Walt Slade is El Halcon?"

"Uh-huh, calls himself Slade, sometimes, anyhow," agreed the deputy.

"But, good gosh, Mark!" old John exploded. "That feller couldn't be El Halcon, the owlhoot! He saved my herd for me over at Bleached Bones Crossing, and risked his own hide to save one of my hands from drowning. Listen while I tell you what happened."

Sullivan listened to the story that came out in a rush of words. He nodded his head sagely when Trout finished.

"Uh-huh, El Halcon does things like that. Sounds just like him. His specialty is horning in on the games of other owlhoots and skimming off the cream. Risking his hide to save another feller's life ain't anything new for him. I don't reckon there's anything that creeps, walks, runs or flies he's scairt of. He'd charge Hell with a bucket of water. Folks say he's got the fastest gunhand in the Southwest. One thing is sure for certain, he's the singingest man in the whole Southwest. Rattlesnakes shed tears and Gila Monsters kiss tarantulas when he cuts loose with that voice of his. But just the same he's plumb bad. Got a heap of killings to answer for."

Ed Block spoke for the first time. "Ever hear of him killing anybody who didn't have a killing coming?"

"Nope," Sullivan admitted. "Reckon that's why he's never stretched rope. He always just saved the sheriff a chore. But give him time and he'll slip; they all do, sooner or later. Where is he? I'd like to say a word to him."

"He — he's gone," old John replied weakly.

"Rode out of town a couple of hours back," Block supplemented.

"Glad to hear it," Sullivan remarked cheerfully. "Can do without him. Too many of his kind mavericking around hereabouts.

62

Well, I'm going to bed. Yes, I'll ride to the Crossing with you tomorrow and pick up those carcasses. Maybe somebody in town will recognize them and maybe give me a line on the rest of the bunch. Be seeing you."

After Sullivan departed, old John turned to his range boss, but with no words of recrimination. Only he said, in a tired voice, "Well, looks like I'll be trying to tie onto that job of riding in a few weeks."

"We'll talk about that tomorrow night," Block countered. "Now what?"

"Now," said Trout, emphatically, "I'm going to get ossified."

"I'm in favor of it," grinned Block, "but for a different reason than you think you got. Barkeep! Fill 'em up!"

Trout and Block proceeded to get ossified with admirable thoroughness. The Lazy K punchers tried their best to keep up, with the result that it was noon the following day when the outfit rode out of Benton, accompanied by Deputy Mark Sullivan, a special, and a couple of mules to pack the bodies of the slain outlaws back to town. Trout was depressed and gloomy, but Block was his usual cheerful self.

They reached the Crossing, and the thicket beside which they left the bodies the day before. Which was all right except for a minor discrepancy: there were no bodies in sight, and a thorough search of the immediate terrain failed to discover any. Sullivan regarded his companions suspiciously.

"Never can tell how drunk a feller is by looking at him," he observed. "That was sure a fine job of imagining you fellers did, John."

"You frazzled end of a misspent life!" roared Trout, his white mustache bristling in his scarlet face. "Do you mean to try and tell me I was lying?"

"Nope, not lying, just imagining," replied the imperturbable deputy.

Trout was about to renew the assault when Ed Block broke in.

"Mark," he said, "what the devil does it mean?"

"It means," the deputy replied soberly, "that somebody was mighty careful to see to it that those carcasses weren't packed to town and put on display. You fellers are sure you never saw either of them before?"

"Yes, we're sure," answered Block.

The deputy swore wearily. "Well, I'll be heading back to town," he said. "Anyhow it was a nice ride. Be seeing you fellers. Take care of yourselves."

The cowboys forded the Pecos without difficulty, the chuck wagon having been left

64

at the railroad stable till the river had gone down. At sunset they began passing over the Lazy K holding. Old John gazed about sadly.

"Seems I know every tree and bush and gulley," he remarked. "Will be a tough tug, uprooting and leaving, yep, it'll be tough." Block smiled and said nothing.

Full dark had fallen when they sighted the ranch-house and other buildings. The bunkhouse was lighted and as they drew near they heard the sound of talk and laughter coming from the building.

"Reckon the wranglers and the boys we left behind are having a little shindig," Trout remarked. "Let 'em enjoy themselves. It's the last they'll have working for me."

Block was about to reply, when the turmoil in the bunkhouse abruptly stilled. And then, a voice, deep and powerful as the roar of the Pecos in its sunken gorge, musical as the wind in the spruces on the hills, soared forth. With one accord the Lazy K riders pulled up to listen as the great golden-baritone-bass pealed and thundered through the starlit night:

Follow the trail of the thundering herd,
With the Texas stars above,
Through the rising mist

65

Of the brown earth kissed
By the frost in his Autumn love!
Follow the trail of dust and dreams,
Where the prairie roses bloom,
Till the coyote prowls
And the lone wolf howls
To his mate in the star-burned gloom!
Follow the gray of the Pecos Trail,
On to the rising sun!
Till the Sabine gleams
In the first red beams,
And the West and the East are one!

The music ended with a ringing crash of guitar cords and was followed by a roar of applause in which the Lazy K riders instinctively joined.

Ed Block grinned at his employer.

" 'The singingest man in the whole Southwest!' " he softly quoted Deputy Mark Sullivan's words.

Old John Trout gave his mustache a vicious tug. Then he succinctly relieved his overcharged feelings:

Well, I'll be hanged!

Six

After putting up their horses, the cowboys trooped into the bunkhouse to receive a hilarious greeting from the two wranglers and three punchers who did not accompany them on the trip. Old John went straight to Slade and drew him aside.

"Here you are, sir," Slade said, passing him the sheaf of bills. "Hadn't you better count it?"

"You go to the devil!" snorted Trout, wadding the money into his pocket. "Son, I want to apologize."

"Apologize? What for?" Slade smiled.

"For doubting you for a minute. I'd ought to have known better; Ed Block went bail for you, and Ed don't make mistakes. I don't give a hang if you're El Halcon or who you are, you're the bully boy with a glass eye for me."

"Thank you, sir," Slade acknowledged, his eyes dancing with amusement. "Who told

67

you I was El Halcon?"

"Deputy Mark Sullivan came spinning a loco yarn about you," replied Trout. "Wait till I see that spavined horned toad! Come on up to the *casa*. We'll all have something to eat and drink. You'll sleep there. First room on the right of the hall at the head of the stairs."

When they entered the big ranchhouse a girl rose from a chair by the fireplace to greet them. She was a very pretty girl, Slade thought, with her hair the color of ripe corn-silk, eyes the hue of the Texas bluebells under a sunny sky, a pert little nose, a creamily tanned complexion and a sweetly turned mouth. She was fairly tall and her figure left nothing to be desired.

"Hello, Dad," she said. "I just got back from the Crickenbergers a little while ago. Everything all right?"

"Yes, everything's all right, thanks to this young feller here," Trout replied. "Honey, this is Walt Slade, the finest jigger that ever spit on the soil. Slade, my daughter Verna."

"For heaven's sake, Dad, watch your language!" she admonished him. "It's nice to know you, Mr. Slade." She extended a little sun-golden hand over which Slade bowed with courtly grace.

"I see you've taken my father in tow," she

said, dimpling up at him.

"He's not very selective and jumps at conclusions, doubtless erroneous ones," Slade smiled.

"You two oughta get along well together," snorted old John. "You both talk like dictionaries. Come along and let's eat, I'm gaunt as a gutted sparrow."

"He's hopeless," Verna said to Slade, "but he means well. Now please don't voice the hackneyed 'road of good intentions' or I'll be disappointed in you."

"I won't," Slade promised, "and in his case I don't think it applies."

"I wanna eat!" bawled old John.

The meal in the big dining room was an enjoyable one. Slade sat next to Verna Trout and they talked together of many things. Ed Block gave a graphic account of the happenings at the Crossing, stressing the part Slade played. Verna shuddered and gazed at Slade with renewed interest.

"No wonder Dad's so smitten with you," she said softly. "I don't blame him. Are you going to sign up with him, Mr. Slade?"

"Possibly, I haven't decided yet," Slade replied. "Want to roam around a few days and take it easy first."

The blue eyes gave him a keen look, but she did not comment and did not pursue the subject further.

Later, in the comfortable room assigned him, Slade unfolded the plat he took from the dead drygulcher's pocket and studied it with an understanding eye.

Shortly before the death of his father, subsequent to business reverses which entailed the loss of the elder Slade's ranch, Walt Slade had graduated from a famous school of engineering. He had contemplated a post graduate course in special subjects to round out his technical education, but that became impossible at the moment. So when Captain Jim McNelty, the famous commander of the Border Battalion, with whom Slade had worked some during summer vacations, suggested that he join the Rangers for a while and continue his studies in spare time, Walt Slade thought it was a good notion. Before so very long he had gotten more by way of private study than he could have hoped for from the postgrad and was all set to enter the profession for which he was trained.

But Ranger work had gotten a strong hold on him and he was loath to sever connections with the illustrious corps of law enforcement officers. He was young. Plenty of time to be an engineer. He would stick with the Rangers for a while. Meanwhile he carefully kept up his studies, familiarizing himself with new methods and developments. And he had more than once found his engineering knowledge invaluable in the course of his Ranger activities. Began to look like the matter in question might be still another example.

For there was no doubt but the plat was a cadastral and topographical survey by the hand of a man who knew his business. The thing looked to be the survey of an elevated tract of land with steep slopes leading up to it. The tie points were marked plainly and definitely. The shape of the outline was peculiar, something like an hourglass some ten miles long by seven or eight across at the widest point, according to the scale, with the lower bulb of the glass to the north and much larger than the southern bulb.

Slade puzzled over a thin, wavy line leading from the west boundary of the survey. Beneath it in small, neatly done block letters was the underscored and cryptic word — POSSIBLE.

A strange thing for a drygulcher to be carrying in his pocket. As strange, Slade mused with a chuckle, as El Halcon packing around forty thousand dollars of another man's money.

Due to his habit of working undercover

71

whenever possible, and often not revealing his Ranger connections, Walt Slade had built up a rather peculiar dual reputation. Those who knew him to be a Ranger held him in high respect — the smartest and most fearless Ranger of them all. Others, including some puzzled sheriffs and other peace officers, were wont to maintain that El Halcon was just an extremely salty and dangerous outlaw who, so far, was too smart to get caught.

Slade did nothing to correct this erroneous viewpoint, although he knew well that it sometimes entailed grave personal danger to himself, as Captain McNelty had more than once reminded him.

"Keep on and some loco trigger-happy sheriff or marshal will be downing you on sight," declared Captain Jim.

"Perhaps," Slade conceded cheerfully. "But because some folks think what they do, there are avenues of information open to me that would be closed to a known peace officer. I'll take a chance, sir, unless you definitely forbid me to."

"Oh, go ahead, if that's the way you feel about it!" growled Captain Jim. "It's your funeral; and that's what it very likely will be sometime — your *funeral!*"

But Walt Slade only chuckled, a dancing

light in his cold, pale eyes, and went on his gay, reckless way with scant worry as to the present and none at all as to the future.

The survey plat continued to be an enigma, so Slade tucked it away and went to bed.

The following morning, after breakfast, old John suggested to Slade that they look over his holdings. Slade offered no objection and they saddled up and set out. It did not take him long to be convinced that the Lazy K was an excellent section of range. There was good grass, plenty of water, thickets and groves to provide shade. Cows were not as plentiful as the land warranted, but Slade gathered that Trout had dipped heavily into his stock to get together the big shipping herd he sold to the railroad.

"I bought more land a while back and sort of overreached myself," Trout said. "You know what the market was last year and the first of this. Things weren't so good. I mortgaged my holding heavily to get the money to invest in more land and good stock for breeding purposes. Have had several extensions of my note, but there's a limit. The banks are loaded with paper right now and the directors and stockholders are getting a mite nervous. Old Matthews Mason, the president, said he couldn't very

73

well carry me any longer. So I combed out about everything worthwhile to fill the fat order the railroad construction folks gave me. You see now why I was so anxious to get that money safe to the ranchhouse, and why saving my herd for me like you did meant so much."

"I see," Slade replied thoughtfully. "Well, you're okay now, aren't you, sir?"

"Yep, I can pay off the note," Trout said. "I'll have to do some scratching for a while to meet necessary expenses, but I'll make out some way. With the big worry off my mind I feel a heck of a sight better. Look over there to the east, son, and tell me if you ever saw anything like that before."

They were approaching a line of high and rocky bluffs with exceedingly steep slopes tumbling down to the prairie. North and south, unbroken, the cliffs, for they were little less, extended for ten or a dozen miles. Opposite where they rode, the cliffs curved inward in a long slant, levelled off, then curved out again. The crest of the big mesa, for as far as the eye could reach, was covered with a comparatively low growth, with occasional tall trees rising above the common level.

"Yes, I've seen quite a number of similar formations, in New Mexico," Slade replied

74

to Trout's question. "New Mexico is famous for its mesas and flat-topped mountains. The mesas over there are also usually covered with trees. Up there appear to be live oaks, most of them not very large."

"That's right," said Trout. "I wonder how the dickens they got there. Not another big stand of live oaks within a couple hundred miles."

"The soil is doubtless of a character favorable to that sort of growth," Slade replied. 'You'll notice that there are a good many tall old trees among the lesser stuff. Seeds from those trees gradually spread over the whole terrain, in the course of years. Doubtless up there are few animals that feed on acorns."

"Guess that's it," agreed Trout. "Anyhow, it's a good deal of a darn nuisance, cluttering up the range like it does. Seven or eight miles to the other side, and the cliffs are the same all the way round. I don't believe there's a place where a horse could make it up to the top."

"It's part of your holding?" Slade asked.

"That's right," answered Trout, "part of what I inherited from my Dad when he passed on. Fact is, it's the reason for me investing in more land. If that hunk of rock was all good range I wouldn't have needed any more acreage."

Slade nodded absently, the concentration furrow deepening slightly between his black brows. The unusual shape of the mesa had an oddly familiar look. He wracked his brain to recall where he had seen a similar formation, and could not. With a shrug he dismissed the matter as of no consequence.

They had been steadily approaching the cliff as they talked, and now they were less than two hundred yards from the thickly brush grown lip that loomed two hundred feet and more above their heads.

"Wonder what ails old fuss-and-feathers up there?" Trout remarked. "He's having a conniption duck fit."

From the growth edging the cliff, a bluejay had suddenly puffballed into the air, screaming and scolding furiously as it wheeled and darted.

Slade's eyes narrowed and were abruptly intent on the fringe of brush above which the jay dipped and fluttered. His concentrated gaze caught a glinting sparkle.

The next instant old John yelped astonishment and alarm as Slade's long arm shot out and swept him from the saddle. Almost as quickly, Slade hit the ground on the far side of his own horse, sliding his Winchester from the saddle boot as he went down.

The bush above which the jay shrieked wisped a trickle of whitish smoke. The jay skyrocketed high in the air at the report. A bullet whizzed through the air, close over the horses' backs.

Slade's Winchester leaped to his shoulder. His eyes glinted along the sights.

The rifle spoke. Slade fired three more quick shots, shifting his aim slightly each time to rake the base of the bush. At the fourth shot the growth was agitated wildly. Something black tumbled out of it and pitched over the lip of the cliff. It was the body of a man. With arms and legs turning in the air it rushed downward to strike the rocks at the base of the cliff with a sodden thud.

"Stay down!" Slade snapped to Trout. "Stay down, there may be another devil up there."

Eyes searching the growth and at the same time noting the movements of the jay, he lay with rifle ready for instant action. The bird, ceasing its scolding, flew lower and lower to finally settle in the bush. It did not rise again.

"He was alone," Slade said, rising to his feet.

Old John also stood up, mopping the sweat which had popped out on his face.

"Son, how the devil did you catch on in time?" he asked.

"I make a habit of watching the movements of birds," Slade explained. "They'll tell you plenty if you'll just pay attention and learn to translate them. A jay doesn't go scooting up in the air that way for no reason. He'd peck the eyes out of a snake that came fooling around his nest, and he'd pay no mind to a coyote or mountain lion, which he'd know wouldn't do him any harm. Something slid under that bush and disturbed him, something he didn't understand and was afraid of. I figured that something could be a man. Then I saw the sun shine on his rifle barrel as he shifted it to line sights, and decided it was time to move."

"You're darn right it was!" sputtered Trout. "I figure that slug went through the air right where one of us was a second before. But why the devil did he shoot at us?"

"That's a question," Slade said. "Let's go see what we bagged."

They walked to the body, which lay face downward on the rocks. Slade turned it over on its back. He glanced up at Trout.

"Recognize him?" he asked.

"Why, blast it!" exclaimed the rancher,

"it's one of the three hellions who were giving us such a close once-over in the Queen High the other night."

"Yes, he was one of them," Slade agreed, his eyes thoughtful.

"You figure he was up there laying for us?" asked Trout.

"Not likely, I'd say," Slade replied. "He'd have hardly guessed we would ride this way today. He was up there for some other reason and saw us riding across the prairie. Watched until we got close enough for him to recognize and decided to take a shot at us."

"Wonder which one of us he was aiming at?" muttered Trout.

"I'd like to know for sure," Slade replied. "But no matter which one he picked out for his first slug, the other would have also gotten it a second later."

Old John mopped his face again. "Son," he said heavily, "I seem to be getting deeper and deeper in your debt all the time. But what was that sidewinder doing up top those rocks? Wonder if there's an owlhoot hangout up there somewhere."

"Not impossible, if there's a place where they can ride up and down," Slade answered.

79

"If there is, I sure don't know it," declared Trout.

Slade nodded, but was not impressed. He doubted if old John had ever given the cliffs a careful examination; there was no reason for him to do so. He resolved sooner or later to have a look at the top of the mesa himself.

Trout glanced at the sun. "It isn't late, and Muerto is only about ten miles to the south," he observed. "Reckon we'd better ride down and let Sheriff Dobson know what happened. While I'm at it, I'll stop at the bank and tell Matthews Mason I'll be in to pick up my note in a day or two. It isn't due for a couple of weeks, but I want to get it off my hands."

Slade paused to turn out the dead drygulcher's pockets, discovering nothing of significance other than considerable money, which he replaced.

"All right, let's go," he said. They mounted their horses and rode south at a good pace. From time to time Slade glanced at the line of cliffs and precipitous slopes that walled the mesa, his brows drawing together, until the rocky wall curved to the east. He shook his head and turned to the front.

Muerto proved to be a sleepy cowtown that hinted at an awakening. Most of the buildings were old, but several new ones were going up. The coming of the railroad was already having its effect.

They hitched their horses to a rack in front of the sheriff's office, which was diagonally across the street from the bank, and entered. A lanky old frontiersman with his boots propped comfortably on a table nodded cordially to Trout and surveyed Slade with disfavor.

"So!" he rumbled. "Heard you were in the section. Still riding around shooting folks, eh? Someday —"

"Some day, Ad, you'll choke to death on your own foot in your mouth," interrupted Trout. "Tighten the latigo on your jaw and listen to what I have to tell you."

The story lost nothing in the telling. "So you see Slade did a pretty good chore of shooting today," he concluded.

"He's always in the clear!" wailed the sheriff. "Nobody can ever get anything on him or make anything stick."

He glowered at Slade, then abruptly his leathery old face split in a grin that made it wonderfully pleasing and youthful. He stuck out a gnarled hand. "Son, no matter what you are, where you come from, or what you've done, saving my old *amigo's* life puts you in plumb solid with me," he said. "I'll shed a tear the day you're hanged."

John Trout chuckled hugely. "Ad's all right," he said, patting the sheriff's shoulder affectionately. "Well, I'm heading for the bank. Come on, Slade."

At the door, Slade glanced back at Sheriff Dobson. The sheriff very deliberately closed one eye.

"Drop in and see me when you get a chance," he said, meaningly.

It was Slade's turn to chuckle. For it was Sheriff Ad Dobson who had written to Captain Jim McNelty, suggesting it would be a good idea to send a few hundred Rangers to the railroad construction area to cramp the style of the outlaw element which was proving too much for the sheriff to handle.

SEVEN

Entering the bank, Trout was heading for a door marked, "President," when a voice hailed him from across the room, "This way, John!"

Seated at a table was an elderly man with a white beard and a pleasant smile.

"Why, hello, Matt," said Trout. "What you doing out here?"

"Tieing up a few last loose ends," the other replied cheerfully. "I'm retiring, John."

"Retiring!"

"That's right. The bank's changed hands, you know. Merged with the Cattleman's Exchange at Pecos. The stockholders and directors thought it was a good move and approved it."

"Well, I'll be darned!" exclaimed Trout. "I knew they were a bit jittery about conditions, but I never thought they'd sell out."

"It was a good offer," said Matthews. "After all, the boys are getting old, like myself, and figured it was about time to hand things over to younger blood. Incidentally, the Cattleman's Exchange has also recently changed hands. An eastern syndicate bought it, I understand."

"Sorry to see you go, Matt, but you've earned a rest," said Trout. "I dropped in to speak about my note the bank holds."

"Ah, yes, the note," nodded Matthews Mason. "Well, John, the bank doesn't own that note any more."

"Doesn't own it?"

"That's right. We sold it right after you asked for an extension."

"I wasn't notified of the sale," protested Trout.

"I would have notified you before the note fell due, as a matter of courtesy," said Mason. "However, the bank was not required to do so. Such a mortgage is negotiable collateral and can be sold, bought, or transferred without the mortgagor being consulted or even notified."

"Who bought it?" asked Trout.

"That fellow who owns a saloon in Benton and is putting up a building to house one here in Muerto," the banker replied. "Name is Richmond Hurst."

"Well, I'll be hanged!" snorted old John. Slade's brows drew together a trifle.

84

"That note of yours seemed to be sort of in demand of late," added Mason. "The day after Hurst bought it, another gent came in and wanted to buy, that man Parks Trimble who opened up a real estate office in Benton about five months back and began getting options on land around Benton, which he has lately been selling at a handsome profit. Seemed sort of put out when we told him the note had already been sold to Hurst."

"I wonder why they wanted to tie onto it?" remarked Trout.

"Oh, I guess they figure this section is up and coming," said Mason. "Be that as it may, as you know, the bank was pretty heavily loaded with paper and when an offer was made for a couple of mortgages the directors were glad to sell."

"Another one sold?"

"That's right. The Randolph mortgage. Randolph owns the ranch next to yours on the west, I believe."

"Yes, he does," nodded Trout.

"I imagine you won't have any trouble talking to Hurst," said the banker. "Appeared to be an amiable sort, a shrewd businessman, all right, but didn't strike me as being unreasonable."

"I don't anticipate any trouble, for I figure to pay off that note right away," said Trout.

"A good idea," nodded Mason. "But come along, I want to introduce you to Jason Gaunt, the manager the Exchange people sent over to take charge here."

He led the way to the door marked "President" and knocked. A voice beyond the panel bade him come in.

Jason Gaunt proved to be a youngish man with keen eyes and a tight mouth. He was slightly above medium height and looked trim and fit. He acknowledged the introductions with a nod and a hand-shake.

"How are you, Mr. Trout?" he said. "I was telling Mr. Mason that I considered the selling of your mortgage a mistake." He hammered the desk top angrily with his fist as he spoke. Slade eyed that slender, immaculately kept hand with interest.

"That's no way to hold business," Gaunt resumed. "I wouldn't have done it. And if you wish to talk business with us again, don't hesitate to come in. I'll always be glad to see you."

"Seems to be a right feller," Trout observed when they were in the outer room again.

"He's all right, but he doesn't understand what a small bank with small capital was up against," replied Mason. "Different with the Cattleman's Exchange, which has large

86

funds to draw on. Well, good luck, John. I'll ride up to see you sometime."

"Do that, Matt," said Trout. "Be glad to have you any time."

Outside the bank, Trout turned to Slade.

"Son, I'm darn glad that, thanks to you, I've got the money to pay off that note," he said. "I've a notion Hurst would foreclose pronto."

"Possibly," Slade conceded, "but I've a feeling that if you were not in a position to pay right now, you'd stand a better chance with Hurst than with Gaunt."

Old John shot him an inquiring glance, but Slade did not amplify the remark and deftly turned the subject.

"I suppose you'll be riding to Benton without delay?" he suggested.

"Tomorrow morning," answered Trout. "And I'd like for you to ride with me."

"I will," Slade promised. "And so will Ed Block and three or four of your hands."

"Huh!" exclaimed Trout. "You figure we might meet with trouble on the way?"

"I figure it's common sense to take precautions against such a possibility," Slade replied grimly.

"And I figure you know what you're talking about, per usual," grunted Trout. "Come on, let's go home."

Slade was unusually silent and preoccupied during the ride back to the ranch-house. He was endeavoring to piece together the illfitting parts of the jigsaw puzzle that confronted him. Why, he wondered, was there such a sudden interest in the Lazy K? It was a good spread, capable of providing a decent living for its owner, but that was all that could be said for it, so far as he had been able to ascertain. But it appeared its ownership was greatly desired in certain quarters. To maintain that two offers to buy up the mortgage in two days was merely coincidence was a bit far-fetched. Slade was of the opinion that there was a very large gentleman of color somewhere in the woodpile, and that it was up to him to root him out.

What intrigued him most and made his interest in the matter imperative was the attempt to destroy John Trout's herd at Bleached Bones Crossing. If Trout had lost his cattle, he would not have been able to meet his note when it fell due. The holder of the note could foreclose. So it appeared that somebody wanted the ranch badly enough to commit murder in an effort to acquire it. Who was that somebody? The finger of suspicion naturally pointed to either Richmond Hurst or the real estate man, Parks Trimble. Slade had contacted Hurst and had held an opinion of him in abeyance. Until today he had never even heard of Parks Trimble. He made up his mind to also contact Trimble at the first opportunity.

Another perplexing angle that must be considered was the attempt to kill Richmond Hurst in the Queen High saloon, a killing that had been prevented, due to Slade's quickness of thought and action, by a hair's breadth. Why did somebody want to kill Hurst? Of course, revenge for some wrong, real or fancied, might have been the motive, although it appeared highly unlikely that such obviously elaborate preparations by a number of individuals would have been made to consummate a grudge killing. The more logical deduction was that Hurst was in somebody's way, or so Slade's Ranger training led him to believe. What that "way" was, he had not the slightest notion.

And what about the little sidewinder who, holed up on top of the mesa, had attempted to drygulch Trout and himself? Where did he fit into the picture? A member of the drygulching bunch at the Crossing, out to even up the score? Possibly, but unlikely. The incident was just another enigma in a pattern of enigmas. At least, he reflected

89

wryly, everything had so far ended in "attempts," but the luck couldn't be expected to hold out forever.

All in all, it seemed that what had appeared to be but a run-of-mine chore of Ranger policing had become a perplexing problem that challenged even El Halcon's ingenuity to solve. And back he came to the initial question, why was somebody so anxious to acquire the Lazy K ranch? Doubtless the answer was right under his nose, could he but see it.

In which he was right. But all too often what lies right under one's nose is too close to properly evaluate and in consequence is overlooked.

Slade abruptly turned to old John.

"And you plan to ride to Benton tomorrow and pay off the note?" he asked.

"That's right," Trout replied, "and you and Ed Block and five or six of the boys are going along, just as you suggested."

"So I wish to ask a favor of you," Slade said.

"It's granted before you ask," replied Trout. "What is it, son?"

"Before you tell Hurst you are ready to pay off the note, I want you to ask him a question."

Old John blinked. "Okay," he said, "what's

the question?"

Slade replied in a single terse sentence. Trout blinked again, but did not hesitate to acquiesce.

"I'll do it," he promised. "I don't know what you've got up your sleeve, but I'll do it."

"I'll tell you later why I want you to ask that question," Slade said. "Hurst's answer may be very important to quite a few people, including yourself."

The following morning, Slade and Trout were sitting in the living room enjoying an after-breakfast smoke when Verna entered.

"Dad," she said, "I'd like to ride with you to Benton today. I'd like to have a look at the town I've heard so much about."

Old John glanced inquiringly at Slade, who nodded slightly. Verna noted the bit of byplay and her eyes flashed. "Okay," her father said. "I'll have your horse made ready." He knocked out his pipe and left the room. Verna turned on Slade.

"It would seem, Mr. Slade, that suddenly one has to obtain your permission to do something," she remarked tartly.

Slade extinguished his cigarette butt, rose to his feet and smiled down at her. "A charming woman is often characterized by a vivid imagination," he said and followed old John to the barn.

Verna glared after him, then abruptly a dimple appeared at the corner of her mouth. She was humming a little tune when she went out to mount her horse.

It was a beautiful early autumn day and the little troop rode at a fast pace. Trout had brought along five hands exclusive of Ed Block, the range boss.

"I figure eight of us can take care of anything we're likely to run into," he said to Slade. "Nine, including Verna; she's a darn good shot."

At the Crossing, Slade called a halt. For some time he sat gazing across the river, which was much lower than on the former occasion, studying the growth which flanked the trail. The hands watched him in silence. Verna fidgeted with impatience. Finally he said, "I believe everything is okay. Miss Verna, you will stay here until the rest of us make the crossing. Weston, you stay with her."

Verna's chin went up. "I'll do nothing of the sort," she declared flatly. "I'm riding with you."

Slade turned and let the full force of his gray eyes rest on her face. "You will stay here until we make the crossing," he repeated, with finality.

"And if I don't, I suppose you'll hogtie me and leave me here!" she exclaimed hotly.

"If necessary."

"Here's my tie rope, son," chuckled old John.

For a moment the blue eyes and the gray locked glances; then abruptly Verna's long lashes fluttered down. "Very well, Mr. Slade," she said meekly.

As they took the water, a young cowboy remarked sententiously to a companion, "Well, if I wore glasses, today I'd throw 'em away, for I've seen everything. I wouldn't have believed there was a man on God's green earth who could make Miss Verna do something she didn't want to."

"That Slade feller has a way with him," the other replied. "If he tells you to do something, I figure it's a good notion to do it."

The crossing was negotiated without incident. Slade turned and waved to Verna and Weston. The others rode on ahead. When the delayed pair reached the bank, Weston spurred to join the others. Slade and Verna brought up the rear. For some minutes they rode in silence, then —

"Mr. Slade," she said, "you have very unpleasant eyes."

"In keeping with my personality, no

93

doubt," he returned.

"And the way you forced me to remain behind was not very courteous."

"Perhaps not, but it was in the interest of your safety."

Her eyes widened a little. "And you really thought somebody might be lying in wait to ambush us?"

"After what happened the other day, I considered it not beyond the realm of possibility, and flying lead plays no favorites," Slade replied.

Again there was silence, then a very small voice said, "I'm sorry. I know I'm just a spoiled brat and used to having my own way. Yes, I'm sorry."

Slade turned to smile at her. "I've a notion it would come natural to any man to spoil you," he said.

At that moment Ed Block came riding back to meet them. "The old man wants to talk to you, Walt," he said.

Slade nodded and rode to overtake Trout. Block reined alongside Verna.

"Ed, just what is he, anyhow?" she asked. "I never before met a man just exactly like him."

"Honey, I don't know," Block replied with the familiarity of many years. "There are folks who say he is an outlaw. Your Dad thinks he's just about God's right-hand man. I've a notion he comes the closest to being right."

"One thing is certain," she said, "trying to trade repartee with him is just a waste of time; you can't win."

"The same goes for trying to trade lead with him," Block replied dryly. A thought seemed to strike him.

"Honey, you getting interested in that young feller?" he asked, a note of apprehension in his voice.

"Ed," she answered, "I was never altogether a fool."

"And what do you mean by that?" demanded the bewildered range boss.

"I mean that any girl who lets herself get seriously interested in him needs her head examined. To him a woman is just something to smile at, to — maybe — kiss, and then forget all about, till the next one comes along."

EIGHT

The way to the Queen High led past the railroad yards. Slade suddenly leaned forward in his saddle and stared. On a nearby siding was a long green and gold private car with "Winona" stenciled on the sides.

"Well, I'll be darned!" he muttered under his breath. "So the Old Man himself is here! Things must not be going just right. This requires a little looking into."

Hitching their horses at a nearby rack, they entered the Queen High in a body. The cowboys headed for the bar. Verna and Ed Block took a table. Slade and Trout walked to where Richmond Hurst stood at the far end of the bar. He greeted them courteously, calling each by name, and shaking hands with Slade.

Old John wasted no time. "Mr. Hurst," he said, "I've come to discuss that note of mine you hold."

"With pleasure," Hurst replied. "Come

96

into the back room, gentlemen; I call it my office. We'll have privacy there."

In the back room they sat down at a table. Hurst called for a bottle and glasses. When the waiter had finished his chore and departed, he looked suggestively at Trout. Old John shot a glance at Slade and then propounded the question Slade had requested him to ask.

"Mr. Hurst," he said, "if I should ask for an extension, would you grant it?"

"Certainly," Hurst replied without hesitation. "I have no desire to squeeze you out, sir. I bought that mortgage as an investment, for I have faith in this section and intend to stay here. I figured that on that mortgage I could lose nothing and might gain considerable. If the time should come when you don't care to take up the note, I'll add what I can afford to the face of it when I take over the property. I've never taken undue advantage of anyone, and I'm getting too old to start now."

Old John looked slightly dazed, Slade very thoughtful.

"Well, that's mighty nice of you, Mr. Hurst," the rancher said. "But I guess I won't have to ask for an extension. If it hadn't been for Slade here, I very likely would have had to, if I'd stayed alive."

"And if it wasn't for Slade, I wouldn't be here to grant you an extension if you asked for it," Hurst said grimly. "Before we discuss the mortgage, let me tell you what happened in here the other night. It's safe to say he never mentioned it to you."

Hurst was a good talker, and the story of the fight in the saloon was portrayed vividly. Old John shook his head.

"Looks like we're both mighty beholden to him," he said when Hurst had finished. "Well, here's your money, Mr. Hurst, and we can tear up the mortgage. If I ever need dinero again, I'll come to you instead of the bank," he added with a chuckle. "Now I want to get something to eat. Talking business always makes me hungry."

Hurst rose to his feet. "If you'll excuse me a few minutes, I'll get the note," he said. "I have it safely put away. That old desk over there is hardly the place to store valuable papers in a fire trap like this building, and I have no strongbox. It will be different at my new place in Muerto. Have another drink till I get back."

With a smile and a nod he left the room, via the back door. Slade and Trout had just finished their drink when he returned with the note.

"Now we'll eat," he said. "Everything on

the house," he added as he led the way to the table. They had almost reached it when he suddenly faltered in his step, his eyes widened, and his face flushed to the hair roots. Slade, glancing at Verna, was sure the color in her cheeks deepened.

"Oh, Lord!" he murmured to himself. "More complications!"

Old John performed the introductions. Hurst bowed over Verna's hand.

"If you don't mind, I'll join you," he said, drawing up a chair. "I haven't had my breakfast yet."

Slade finished eating first. He stood up, rolling a cigarette. "Have a little chore I want to attend to," he told Trout. "Be back shortly."

"Take your time," said old John. "It's comfortable here, and I can stand another snort or two."

Verna, who was deep in conversation with Richmond Hurst, nodded and smiled. Slade sauntered out the door.

In his private car, James G. "Jaggers" Dunn, the famous general manager and builder of the great C. & P. railroad system, sat glowering at the papers littering his desk. Sam, his porter, chef, and general factotum, hovered about making clucking noises indicative of

99

sympathy with his master's mood.

From the street paralleling the siding came a chorus of wild yells and a stutter of shots. Jaggers Dunn, who knew it was only a bunch of cowboys skylarking into town, did not look up from his desk. Sam didn't know that and his eyes rolled apprehensively white in his black face. He peered out the window and saw a tall, broad-shouldered man who wore two guns striding toward the back steps of the car.

"Oh, Lawdy! Lawdy!" he exclaimed. "Here comes ol' Jesse James hisself! Now we'll all get shot!"

Dunn glanced out absently, stared, craned his neck. He leaped to his feet with a lion-like roar. Brushing the chattering Sam aside, he flung open the door and bellowed a greeting.

"Slade! By all that's holy, if this isn't luck! Come in! Come in! Sam, break out a bottle, one of my personal ones I tell you not to take swigs out of, and bring glasses. Slade, you're a life-saver if there ever was one. Sit down here and have a drink; then we'll talk."

"And now what's got you all worked up, sir?" Slade asked as he sampled Dunn's excellent bourbon. "Something wrong?"

"There's plenty wrong," growled the general manager. "My construction engineer, Lafe Whittaker, disappeared ten days ago. Vanished in thin air. Not a hide or hair of him seen since. Rutledge, the engineer in charge of the project, wired me three days ago. I hurried over here and Rutledge confirmed his wire. And there's not a competent man I can tie onto in a hurry to fill Whittaker's place."

"Think something — happened to him?" Slade asked. Dunn drummed the desk top with his finger a moment before replying.

"I'd hesitate to level such a charge at my competition, the M. K.," he said at length. "They are ruthless and predatory in their financial manipulations and good at taking short cuts, but I'd be loath to think they'd resort to kidnaping or murder to further their ends."

"The M. K. might have nothing to do with what could have happened to Whittaker," Slade pointed out. "This is a rough, raw country, sir, and it's easy for a man to get into trouble of one sort or another."

"I agree with you there," said Dunn. "I learned from Rutledge that Whittaker was a heavy drinker and gambled."

"Drinking and gambling provide an easy road to trouble in this section," Slade interpolated.

"That's right," nodded Dunn. "I'm of the

opinion that he might possibly just have gone on a bender after he completed the bridge job. Rutledge hired him while I was in Europe, after Jim Bates came down with the fever and died. Rutledge said he was excellently recommended and was undoubtedly a competent bridge and grade man. Be that as it may, he's gone. Which brings me to the nubbin of the ear. I'm worried about that bridge. It may well be the key to the race for the coast. We got the jump on the M. K. there. They've just started their bridge, and they're having trouble. Rutledge is confident the bridge is okay — he's got rails laid across it and everything — but old Cassidy, the foreman of the masons, appears bothered about it. He's not an engineer, but he knows masonry and has had a great deal of experience in bridge building. He doesn't seem to know what's wrong, but he's bothered. You know the kind, have a feel for things but can't explain just why they feel that way. Anyhow, he's got me worried. So I want you to ride down to that bridge right away. Give things a thorough going over and report back to me what your opinion is."

"Hold on, sir," Slade said laughingly. "I'm a Ranger, not a railroad builder."

"Yes, and you're also one of the best

engineers in the business," Dunn retorted. "You've helped me out before, and you've got to do it now. I'll fix things with McNelty."

"Oh, all right," Slade capitulated. "I know from past experience that if there's anything off-color going on in a section where it runs, your darned railroad is mighty liable to be mixed up in the middle of it. Wouldn't be surprised if that's the case here. I'm staying in town tonight. I'd planned to ride back tomorrow to his ranch west of the river with a friend of mine, but I'll put that off and have a look-see at your bridge. Chances are you're just borrowing trouble over that bridge."

"Maybe so," grunted Dunn, "but I've got about as much Irish blood as Cassidy and the same knack of sniffing out trouble, and right now I sure smell a rat."

Slade chuckled and didn't argue the point.

"Want Rutledge to ride down there with you?" the general manager asked.

Slade thought a moment, then shook his head. "No," he replied, "and don't tell him anything about me. But I'd like for him to be on the spot when I get there. Tell you what, things being as they are in this section, I think it would be a good idea to have that bridge guarded day and night, until your steel reaches it. Have Rutledge take a gang of men down there to choose the best location for a shack to house the guards. Impress on him the importance of the move; that will be ample excuse for sending him."

"Okay, I'll take care of it," Dunn nodded. "I'll have him start from the railhead with wagons and materials first thing in the morning."

Slade went back to the Queen High, where he found his companions still at the table. Old John was drinking and smoking and conversing with Block. Verna and Richmond Hurst appeared to still find plenty to discuss. Old John knocked out his pipe.

"Suppose you and I amble down to the Bear Cat for a look-see," he suggested. "I think the boys have moved down there."

Slade was agreeable and they left the Queen High. Old John chuckled as they passed through the swinging doors.

"That Hurst jigger 'pears to be considerable of a feller," he remarked.

"He does," Slade agreed. Or, he reflected, an extremely smooth and shrewd article who might have instantly divined that Trout had come to pay off the note and reacted accordingly. His definite judgment of Mr.

Richmond Hurst must still be held in abeyance for a while.

They found the Lazy K cowboys playing poker at the Bear Cat. Trout expressed a desire to join the game.

"Block can look after Verna," he said. "I told him to sign up for quarters for all of us at the hotel. We might as well enjoy ourselves while we got the chance."

Slade agreed. He informed Trout that he proposed to remain in town for a day or two and promised to return to the ranchhouse soon.

The poker game lasted until late, but Slade was up early the following morning. He had breakfast with Jaggers Dunn in the railroad magnate's private car, then rode south by west, arriving at the site of the bridge about ten in the morning.

The massive structure was located a couple of hundred yards below where the river made a sharp bend. Slade sat studying the bridge and its approaches with eyes that missed nothing. He gazed at the angry water frothing and dashing against the west and middle piers, followed the course of the river upstream to the bend, where the east bank was formed by low, beetling cliffs against which the current slammed to bounce back like a living thing and go diagonalling southward in a welter of foam and tossing ripples. The concentration furrow deepened between his black brows.

Nearby a gang of men were already busy erecting a shack to house the proposed guards. Superintending the activities was a small, pleasant-faced man of middle age. He kept casting curious glances at Slade. Finally he left the scene of operations to saunter to the river bank and paused beside Shadow.

"Howdy, cowboy?" he greeted. "Looking things over?"

"Somewhat," Slade replied. "You are Mr. Rutledge, I presume?"

"Why, yes," replied the engineer in surprised tones.

"I'd like to ask you a question, sir," Slade said. "Are you familiar with this river and the country through which it runs, especially to the north of here?"

"Why, no," Rutledge replied, "but Mr. Whittaker, who built the bridge, was thoroughly familiar with both."

"He was an engineer?" Slade asked curiously.

"An extremely able one," Rutledge replied with a smile. "Otherwise he could hardly have erected that bridge. Why do you ask?"

"I thought perhaps he was a carpenter,"

Slade drawled.

Rutledge bristled a little at this implied slur to a member of his profession.

"Mr. Whittaker was a very competent engineer who was highly recommended by his former employer," he said crisply.

"And who was his former employer?"

"The N. O. & E. Railroad, sir."

Slade let his gaze drop to the engineer's face, and there was a hard glitter in the depths of his gray eyes.

"And am I to presume, sir, that you are aware that the N. O. & E. is an eastern subsidiary of the M. K. railroad system?"

Rutledge blinked dazely "Why — why — no," he sputtered. Slade believed him.

"The M. K. owns the N. O. & E. lock, stock and barrel," he said.

Rutledge gaped at him. "Just who are you, and what are you getting at?" he demanded.

"You'll find out later," Slade told him. He whirled Shadow and sent him racing north by east, leaving the little engineer staring after him in slack-jawed bewilderment.

NINE

Shadow was pretty well lathered when Slade pulled him to a halt beside Dunn's private car but otherwise didn't appear much affected by the more than a dozen miles he had covered at top speed.

Dunn was at his desk when Slade entered. "Well?" he asked, looking up.

Slade sat down and began rolling a cigarette. "Well," he said, "I want you to pull every mason and sandhog you've got off the job and send them down to the bridge, along with as many more as you can hire. I want cut stone, lots of it, big blocks, and cribbing for coffer dams. I want plenty of dynamite, and several good powder men — I'll need a good many thousand tons of broken rock before I've finished — and fifty or sixty laborers, and all necessary machinery. Arrange for temporary housing for the workers; they'll be there for a while."

"Good Lord!" exclaimed the general

108

manager. "What's up?"

"Your bridge is, at the moment, but it won't be if something isn't done in a hurry. Suppose you get things moving, sir, and then I'll explain."

There was a telegraph instrument hooked up in the private car. Dunn, a skilled telegrapher, began clicking out messages that scorched the wires.

"Now suppose you tell me what's in the wind," he said as he closed the key and turned back to Slade.

"You've been taken, sir," Slade replied. "No wonder Whittaker disappeared as soon as he'd finished work on the bridge. He was planted by the M. K. Came from the N. O. & E., which, as of course you know, is a recently acquired feeder of the M. K. He did a fine job of building, for the M. K. The piers are not nearly wide enough at the base. They are not high enough; during a bad flood your tracks would be under water. I only hope they're anchored on bedrock and not shifting sand, but I'm afraid they're not. We'll have to put shoring under the span, jack it up and heighten the piers. Maybe we won't have to tear them down; with good coffer dams we may be able to work from the bottom. And that's not the worst of it. At the bend of the river, the

109

mouth of a canyon, to the north of the bridge, the current bangs against the cliffs, bounces back and heads straight for the center and west piers. No breakwaters were constructed. We'll have to build them, for a really bad rain up at the headwaters of the Pecos will send down a volume of water that'll take that bridge out as if it were so much straw."

Jaggers Dunn raised both fists above his head and swore until he was blue in the face.

"I'll fire Rutledge for hiring that scoundrel!" he roared.

"No sense in taking it out on Rutledge," Slade said. "He had no reason to believe Whittaker other than what he claimed to be — a competent engineer who specialized in bridge work and with excellent credentials. The average engineer, unacquainted with this section of the country and the vagaries of the Pecos, would pronounce that bridge a fine piece of construction. And Rutledge could not be expected to know that the N. O. & E. is an M. K. subsidiary. I wouldn't have known it myself if I hadn't been interested in your railroad and when I was ordered here, I briefed a bit on the M. K. In that system's 'biography' is an inconspicuous item mentioning the M. K. acquisition of the N. O. & E., a small feeder in Louisiana

110

and Georgia. I remembered it, and when Rutledge mentioned the N.O. & E. as Whittaker's reference, it came to mind."

"Seems to me Rutledge should have noticed high water marks and realized the thing Whittaker was putting up wouldn't hold," growled Dunn.

"There are high water marks left when the river is swollen by the melting snows in spring and the fall rains," Slade replied. "But the flash floods that roar down it now and then leave no high water marks. They're gone within an hour. Quite likely an experienced bridge engineer might have noticed things that would have possibly made him suspicious of the river and caused him to investigate thoroughly. Whittaker didn't need to do any investigating; he already *knew.* It's a strange river, the Pecos. At an upper point it may be almost dry, while at its mouth it's pouring four hundred thousand cubic feet of water a second into the Rio Grande. The name of another Rio Grande tributary would suit it better — Devil's River."

"I believe you've got the right of it," grunted Dunn. "One thing is sure for certain, if I ever get my hands on that blasted Whittaker I'll skin him up till he'll look like the American Flag."

Slade nodded without comment. He did not think Jaggers Dunn would ever lay hands on Whittaker. For it was his opinion that Lafe Whittaker was dead.

"Men and materials will be headed for the bridge within an hour," said Dunn. "I gave orders that work be carried on day and night till the shelters are erected. The cut stone and everything else you asked for will be on their way without delay. The wagons will be ready for transport from the railhead. Anything else you want?"

"Yes," Slade replied. "Absolute authority."

"You'll get it," growled Jaggers. He seized pen and paper and dashed off a single sentence in a handwriting that looked like a barbed wire railing and appended his signature, once seen, never forgotten.

"Guess that will hold you," he said, passing the paper to Slade.

"Guess it will," Slade smiled. He folded the sheet and stowed it away.

"And now, let's have something to eat," said Dunn. "Sam! rustle your hocks!"

"I'll take care of my horse first," Slade answered. "I think I'll ride down there again today; should be able to make it by dark."

"You've already done about thirty miles in the saddle," Jaggers protested.

"A little more won't hurt me, or Shadow,"

Slade replied cheerfully, and left the car.

It was growing quite dark when Slade pulled up at a scene of hectic activity around the bridge head. Flares and bonfires made the area bright as day. Shovels scraped, picks thudded, hammers tapped. An apparently endless stream of huge wagons loaded with various materials rolled down from the northeast. And creating order from what appeared to be utter chaos, was an extremely competent and energetic Dave Rutledge, engineer in chief for construction of the C. & P. Railroad. He spotted Slade immediately and strode across to him.

"Well, young man," he said, "I am of the opinion that you are responsible for all this."

"Yes, I'm afraid I am," Slade smiled.

"Would you mind telling me what it is all about?" asked Rutledge. "Mr. Dunn's orders were very precise, but he didn't explain; he seldom does."

Slade told him, in detail. Rutledge shook his head in astonishment. "And so Whittaker was a plant for the M. K.," he muttered. "I suppose Mr. Dunn considers me a bumbling incompetent for letting him put it over on me like that."

"He does not," Slade replied. "Mr. Dunn's regard for you has not lessened. He knows very well that the same thing could have happened to him. It could have happened to anybody not familiar with this section and the utterly unpredictable manner in which the Pecos cuts up."

"You saw through it at once," Rutledge pointed out.

"Because I am familiar with all I mentioned," Slade replied.

"You are evidently an engineer," Rutledge remarked.

"I am not certificated," Slade replied with a smile. "But I do know a little about the principles of engineering."

"An outstanding example of understatement, I'd say," Rutledge observed dryly. "Is Mr. Dunn coming down to give the orders?"

Slade smiled and shook his head. Without speaking, he passed a folded sheet to the engineer. The bewildered Rutledge read:

All officers and employees of the C. & P. railroad system will obey orders given by the bearer, Walter J. Slade, without question, to the letter, and at once.

James G. Dunn
General Manager and Vice-President
for Operation.

"Well!" gasped Rutledge. "Nothing like

this ever happened to me before."

"Circumstances are a bit unusual," Slade replied, with a smile. "Is Cassidy, the mason foreman, here?"

"Yes, he's here, and his whole gang with him," Rutledge replied. "And all the sand hogs, and a crew of carpenters, and sixty-five laborers, and more coming. Everybody's busy erecting the shacks, right now, and a cook shanty."

"I want to see Cassidy," Slade said.

Rutledge led the way to where a big, red-headed man of middle age was superintending the erection of the cook shanty. Two cooks had already set up business in the open and had built fires under various cooking utensils, including huge boilers of coffee.

"This is Cassidy," said Rutledge. "Cassidy, this is Mr. Slade, who will be in charge from now on."

"Until a decent bridge is erected," Slade corrected smilingly.

Cassidy touched his cap with a brawny hand. Tall as he was, he had to raise his eyes to meet Slade's level gray gaze.

"I'm glad to hear it, sir," he said. "That bridge gives me a sort of sick feeling every time I look at it."

"Cassidy," Slade said, "I believe you

handled the masonry of those piers?"

"That's right, sir," the big fellow answered.

"Are they seated on bedrock?"

"They are not," Cassidy replied. "They are seated on hard packed sand. I mentioned to Mr. Whittaker that I doubted if the sand would hold, come a bad rise of water. He told me to hold my tongue and leave such matters to wiser heads. I shut up, for he was the boss. He said the sand would hold."

"Mr. Whittaker was a liar," Slade said dispassionately. "How far down to bedrock?"

"About ten feet, sir."

"Very well," Slade said. "We will anchor those piers on bedrock. I don't think it will be necessary to tear them down. We will work one side at a time, after the coffer dams are built around them. Pump out the sand and work the masonry into place. Keep on going around, side by side, and repeat the process until bedrock is reached. Also, the piers will have to be heightened at least two feet. Have piling driven, and I want it driven to bedrock, place jacks and raise the spans. Then build the piers to the required height. You can handle that chore?"

"Yes, sir, I can handle it," Cassidy said. Slade did not doubt that he could.

"We will build breakwaters just this side of the bend, to shunt the current between the piers instead of against them as is the condition at present. This is a job that will have to be done fast. It's the time of year for bad rains up around the Pecos headwaters. If a big flash flood comes down before we're finished, there won't be any bridge. And, incidentally, the C. & P. will very likely lose the race to the coast in consequence."

"We'll do it, sir," Cassidy declared grimly. "We'll do it."

"All the necessary machinery is on the way," Slade said, "and if I know Mr. Dunn, it won't be long until we have it to hand. That will be all for tonight, Cassidy, and after you eat you had better get some sleep. The carpenters can handle what's needed at present. Get some rest, for from now on you are construction foreman in charge."

"Yes, sir!" said Cassidy, a grin splitting his leathery countenance. "Thank you, sir."

"I'm depending on you," Slade said.

"You can, sir," Cassidy declared and hurried away.

"Mr. Slade, I think you know how to pick men," Rutledge observed. "And how to handle them," he added.

"I hope so," Slade said. "Now I want you

to get back to the railhead. You have a horse here?"

"Yes, I have a horse, but Mr. Dunn sent word for me to stay here until he recalled me."

"Don't let that bother you," Slade replied. "I'm sending you back to the railhead. I want you to lay steel like you've never laid steel before. Every hundred yards gained will expedite the work here. Good luck to you."

The engineer departed, shaking his head. Slade chuckled. He had sized up Rutledge as a competent man and an honest one. Things would pick up at the railhead as soon as he arrived there, although at the moment he hardly knew which end he was standing on.

Slade got the rig off Shadow and turned him loose to graze in comfort. Then he spread his blanket under a tree and arranged his saddle for a pillow. For some time he watched the work on the shanties, then, satisfied that everything was going smoothly, stretched out on the blanket and despite the problems that cluttered his mind, was almost instantly asleep.

Ten

Dawn was streaking the east with primrose and gold when Slade awoke. All around, men who had labored most of the night lay in sodden sleep; any place they could lay their heads was bed enough for those hardy toilers. But more had arrived during the night to take their place and the activity around the bridge head was unabated. The shacks were nearing completion and from the cook shanty that lacked only a roof came the appetizing aroma of frying meat and boiling coffee. Pile drivers had arrived and were ready to set in place the wagonloads of forty-foot piling.

The word had gotten around, and when Slade joined the workers for breakfast he was greeted with grins and nods and waving of hands. He had swallowed a last cup of steaming coffee when a delegation of the workers waited on him.

"Mr. Slade," said the brawny spokesman,

"the boys would be after asking a favor of you."

"Anything I can grant," Slade replied. "What is it?"

"Sir, the boys would be after liking it a great deal if after we knock off tonight, you'd sing 'em a song or two. Lopez here has a guitar."

"How do you know I can sing?" Slade asked gravely, but with a dancing light in his eyes.

"Begorry! and who doesn't that El Halcon can sing like — like he shoots!" grinned the spokesman.

"Okay," Slade promised, "I'll do it."

"And now, sir, the boys will build you a bridge you can run the Washington Monument across on wheels, or my name ain't Tim Rafferty!" the spokesman declared. A cheer went up and the men scattered to take up their various chores.

"And we'll beat those M. K. scuts to the coast, never fear," Rafferty said in parting.

After breakfast the real work on the bridge began. The pile drivers were placed and began hammering the piling into the river bed until they thudded solidly on bedrock. On the tops of the clusters of piles, massive timbers would be spiked and bolted to support the huge hydraulic jacks that would raise the bridge spans to the required height. The boom of dynamite blasts sounded from where the powder men were blowing down the cliffs to the north to provide broken stone for the breakwaters. The sand hogs were busy preparing to build the coffer dams around the piers, and pumps were ready to draw off the water inside the dams and suck out the sand from beneath the piers so that the masonry could be extended to the bedrock beneath the present unstable pier foundations.

About mid afternoon Jaggers Dunn himself arrived on the scene, via a buckboard. He shook hands with Slade, hauled off his hat and brushed back his glorious crinkly white mane from his big dome-shaped forehead.

"See you've got things moving," he said.

"Yes, they're moving," Slade answered. "The boys are working like devils with no pitch hot."

"Tell them that when they get this infernal bridge anchored as it should be there'll be a bonus for every man jack," said Dunn, adding, "and payday isn't far off. They can have a bust that is a bust."

"And the last one in Benton, no doubt," Slade observed. Jaggers shot him a quick look.

"And what do you mean by that?" he asked.

"Not going to make Benton your General Division point and junction for the southern line, are you?" Slade countered.

"Don't miss a bet, do you?" Jaggers grunted. "No, Benton is not going to be Division. We let the impression be given that it was, so that land values wouldn't sky-rocket around Muerto to the west, which will be Division. Why'd you bring that up?"

"Because I think there has been a leak," Slade replied. "I think some folks know very well that Muerto and not Benton will be Division."

"The devil you say!"

"Oh, it's not common property," Slade replied, "but I'm pretty sure that at least two men either guessed what was in the wind or had inside information."

"Who?" demanded Jaggers.

"Richmond Hurst, who runs the Queen High saloon in Benton, for one. He's setting up a big and very elaborate place in Muerto, which he certainly wouldn't have done if he expected Muerto to remain the sort of a cattle town it's been for fifty years."

Jaggers Dunn muttered an oath. "And who's the other one?" he asked.

"A fellow named Parks Trimble who has a

real estate office in Benton. He showed up there when Benton was just another cow town similar to Muerto, before the road reached Benton and turned it into a construction town. He started off right away getting options on land around Benton, or so I was informed, and has of late been selling what he calls 'town lots' like hot cakes. Why? Because he knew from the beginning that Benton was not going to be Division. He bought low. Then when people began assuming that Benton would be Division and grow, he unloaded at a nice profit. Buy low, sell high! A shrewd operator who isn't bothered by conscience."

"Try to protect your own interests against the unscrupulous and you open up a road for some rascal to travel on and take advantage of others," growled Jaggers, who *was* bothered by a conscience.

"Too late to do anything about it now," Slade said.

"I'm afraid you're right," Dunn agreed morosely. "Well, I'm going back to the railhead and keep your supplies rolling. Any orders?"

"Well, if you're in that mood," Slade grinned, "I would suggest that you keep in touch, by telegraph, with San Jose up near the headwaters of the Pecos and learn if it starts to rain up there — about the time of the year for some bad ones. If flood water heads this way, the sooner I know and can take steps against it, the better off I'll be."

"I'll do it," Dunn promised. "Anything else?"

Slade hesitated a moment, then —

"You'd be doing me a favor, sir, if you would try and find out who is the new owner of the Cattleman's Exchange Bank at Pecos. I was told it was recently sold to an eastern syndicate. If you can find out the composition of that syndicate, what interests it consists of, it may help me to clear up a strange and complicated mess here, the exact nature of which I am not yet sure but which I feel is sinister."

"Okay, I'll do the best I can for you," Dunn said. "That all? Yes? Well, *adios!*" He turned the buckboard and drove north by east.

The work went on apace. Slowly the ponderous breakwaters crept out into the river as the powder men brought down tons of broken stone. The coffer dams, firmly anchored by piling, took form. Soon they would be ready for the pumps which would draw the water from inside the dams. Carloads of cut stone had arrived via twenty-mule-team wagons. The jacks were in place to raise the spans as soon as the piers were solidly anchored on bedrock. The spans would be left in place until that most difficult of the chores was completed, to minimize the chance of sideways slipping by the piers.

Slade was everywhere. He did not hold back from any task and was continually as muddy and wet as the lowliest sand hogs working in the reek of the river bed.

"Aye, he's a man to work for," declared big Tim Rafferty, the foreman of the sand hogs. "He don't stand back and say, 'go ahead, boys!' He's right there in front hollerin' '*come* along, boys!' That one word makes a devil of a difference!"

Finally the coffer dams were completed and pumped out, and the most hazardous portion of the undertaking was at hand. With smoking flares to light them, the sand hogs toiled in the murky depths, levering the ponderous blocks of cut stone into place as the pumps sucked out the supporting sand. Around and around the piers they maneuvered, taking the greatest care to make sure the pier always had sufficient support to hold it level, for a slip would be fatal to the tall truncated irregular cone, and perhaps to the men working in the shadow of its enormous bulk.

"It's one devil of a job, sir," Cassidy said to Slade as they stood on the edge of the central dam, gazing down at the flickering shadows far below. "The boys are taking a chance every minute they're down there."

Slade nodded. He knew Jaggers Dunn would back up any decision he made. He leaned over and his great voice thundered down the shaft —

"Every hour put in down in these holes will be at double time! That's right! Double money!"

From the shadows beneath rose a muffled cheer —

"Hurrah for the Old Man!"

Cassidy chuckled with delight. "And if you were ninety, those hellions wouldn't call you the 'Old Man' if they didn't figure you a boss worth working for," he declared. "You've got 'em, sir! Just keep on singing to them every night like you do, and if you ask it, they'll raise Hell on stilts and put out the fire!"

The very next day, tragedy struck. The central pier was much the most difficult to work. Despite the tightness of its construction and the firmness of the anchorage, water seeped into the dam and the sand beneath the pier steadily grew more fluid, increasing the tendency to a sideways slip.

The task of forcing the great stone blocks into position steadily became more difficult and dangerous.

Slade knew this, and spent all the time he could spare around the central pier. He and Cassidy were standing on the edge of the dam when from the noisome depths came a scream, a shriek of pain and fright followed by another and another, oddly muffled. A chorus of shouts and curses arose.

"What's the matter down there?" Slade roared.

"A rock slipped and caught Gilhooley under it!" Rafferty bellowed back. "It's slipping and crushing him. We can't get him out!"

"Stay here," Slade told Cassidy. He went down the ladder hand over hand, dropping the last ten feet to the ooze and muck. The flares showed the legs and body of the trapped man writhing frantically. His head and shoulders were under the stone block that weighed fully a thousand pounds. His fellow workers were striving frantically to stay its progress as it inexorably pressed Gilhooley into the sand. Despite their efforts, it continued to move forward, slow fraction of an inch by slow fraction of an inch.

Slade took in the situation at a glance. "Cassidy!" he shouted to the masonry foreman. "Cassidy, get a couple of jacks, quick. Lower them by ropes."

"They'll never get here in time," muttered Rafferty.

"Maybe not, but maybe they will," Slade replied, measuring the distance from the stone to the dam timbers. "When they get here, set the bases against the timbers of the dam, the heads against the stone, and drive it back. I'll try and hold it till they get here. Out of the way!"

He stretched out in the mud and water, braced his feet against the dam timbers, slowly lowered his body until his back and shoulders were against the block of stone and stretched to almost his full length.

"Man! you can't do it!" yelled Rafferty. "You'll just get yourself killed. We'll all be killed if the pier topples."

"Anybody who wants to can get out," Slade panted as the sliding stone pressed harder and harder against his shoulders. "But I'll need four volunteers to handle the jacks."

Not a man moved from his place.

Harder and harder pressed the stone. Slade lay rigid, his body unyielding as a bar of steel. The strain grew terrific. His limbs shook as with ague, his breath came in gasps. *But the stone had stopped sliding!*

Slowly the minutes passed. The sand hogs stood helpless, for there was not room for more than one man to brace against the block. Slade knew he couldn't stand the awful strain much longer. His muscles seemed turning to water. The screams of the trapped man had died to gurgling moans. His body no longer moved.

A bubbly mist was forming before Slade's eyes, alternated by flashes of reddish light. His temples throbbed and pounded. There was an iron band constricting his chest, so that he could not breathe. His strength was ebbing fast, but to relax for an instant would mean Gilhooley's death. And very likely his own if the stone surged forward to strike him with full force. The dragging minutes passed. He could hear Rafferty muttering prayers to the saints, his fingers working as if he told the beads of a Rosary.

Suddenly, as from a great distance, he dimly heard shouts above. Down came the jacks, bumping and scraping against the timbers. Brawny arms seized them, set them in place, worked the levers madly. Slade abruptly felt the pressure on his shoulders ease slightly as the heads clamped against the stone.

"We've got it, sir!" shouted Rafferty. "Come out! Come out!"

Slade relaxed, rejoicing in a relief to his tortured muscles that was almost intolerable. He rolled aside and for several moments lay breathing in great gulps. Then he got to his feet, shakily, and smiled wanly. Gilhooley was being dug from under the stone. He was unconscious but still breathing.

Big Rafferty straightened up and gazed at Slade. He stuck out his hand.

"Sir," he said solemnly, "I'd be honored if you would shake. I've worked with many a raunching good man in my time, but never a man like you! Never a man like you!" He gripped Slade's hand and whirled to the sand hogs.

"All together, you terriers!" he bawled — *"Hurrah for the Old Man!"*

Eleven

A hastily improvised sling was lowered, the unconscious Gilhooley sent aloft in it.

"Don't think he's seriously injured," Slade said. "Bad head and face bruises are about all, I'd say. Fainted from strain and exhaustion."

With a nod, he slowly climbed the ladder in the wake of the sling. The sand hogs began working the recalitrant stone back into place and preparing to set another.

Slade was sipping coffee in the cook shanty when a horseman rode up with a message from Jaggers Dunn. It read:

"Raining at San Jose."

The day shift was just trooping in to eat, the night shift preparing to go on duty. Slade called the men together.

"We've got to drill, boys," he told them. "Raining up at the headwaters of the Pecos.

131

We'll have flood water here before long."

A dozen voices shouted reply, "We'll do it, sir! We'll do it."

The tempo quickened. Dynamite boomed. Sledges thudded. With bangings and splashings, broken stone poured onto the breakwaters. Cranes chattered as they lowered the massive blocks of stone into the coffers. And far below the surface of the river, in mud and water, the sand hogs toiled ceaselessly. Slade slept a few hours and was back on the job while it was still dark. About mid morning another message came down from the railhead:

"Raining at Dixon, a hundred miles south of San Jose. Raining hard. Storm appears to be traveling southward."

Slade read the message and shook his head. "We're going to catch it," he told Cassidy. "A steady rise doesn't bother me much, with the breakwaters as far out as they are. What we've got to watch out for is a sudden heavy downpour that will start a flash flood. Before that happens, if it does, we *must* have the piers set and the spans resting on them."

"We'll do it," declared Cassidy. "I'm going to talk with the boys."

Slade nodded and gazed northward, to where railhead was now plainly in view, the swarm of workers looking like a nest of disturbed ants. The wagon haul was now very short, which helped. He glanced at the stacks of cut stone, estimated that very little more would be needed. Stone for the breakwaters was coming down at a satisfactory rate. A little more time and the chore would be whipped. Now everything depended on what came down from the lowering heavens.

In less than forty-eight hours from the receipt of the first message, the rain was making itself felt. The Pecos' growl and grumble through the canyon to the north took on a more strident note. The color of the water had changed; now it had an ominous yellow tinge. The river was rising, slowly but steadily. Slade estimated that another thirty-six hours would bring it to a dangerous level. But within thirty-six hours, nothing going wrong, the bridge should be in shape to resist high water. A flash flood would be something else, but just a few additional hours and he believed the spans could cope with even that eventuality.

That afternoon, Slade had visitors. Old John Trout and Verna rode up to the bridge.

"So here you are!" chuckled the rancher.

"A railroad builder as well as a cowhand, eh?"

"Sort of, for the time being," Slade conceded, smiling at Verna, who smiled back.

"We rode to Benton to find out what was holding you up," Trout explained. "Richmond Hurst told us where you were and what you were doing, so we ambled down for a look. 'Pear to be having quite a time here."

"We'll have more of a time if this blasted river keeps on rising," Slade predicted, a trifle grimly.

"Liable to get bad," Trout said. "I know the old Pecos and what she's capable of. Turns into the Mississippi on a drunk overnight. But Hurst says you'll lick it."

"I hope so," Slade replied. "How is Hurst?"

"He's okay," nodded Trout. "Couldn't talk enough about you. He promised to ride back to the ranch with us tomorrow. Says he'd like to look the spread over. Sort of intimated that, later, he might turn from liquor selling to cow raising; 'pears to know plenty about it."

Slade shot Verna a glance. Her lashes fluttered down and she colored prettily. Slade drew a deep breath. "Light off and have some coffee and a snack," he invited. "We've

134

got a good cook. Couple of them, in fact."

"Not a bad notion," acceded Trout. "Riding always makes me hungry. When do you expect to be over to the spread, son?"

"After the bridge is anchored in place," Slade replied. "That is, if the Pecos doesn't head it for the Rio Grande and the Gulf of Mexico."

"I ain't betting on the Pecos," Trout declared cheerfully. "How about you, Verna?"

"I'm not betting against anything Mr. Slade undertakes," the girl replied, with emphasis.

"You might get a surprise," Slade said, his eyes dancing.

"I could stand one, but I don't expect to get it," she flashed back at him. Slade thought that one over and felt it best to change the topic of conversation.

As old John and his attractive daughter rode away, some time later, Slade gazed after them with puckered brows. There was no doubt in his mind but that Richmond Hurst was badly smitten with the girl, and it was not unlikely that she would reciprocate; Hurst could be very charming when he took a notion to be. Slade liked Verna Trout and didn't want to see her get hurt. And he still hadn't made up his mind about

Richmond Hurst. He admitted that Hurst, as a person, had made a favorable impression on him, but to all appearances he was embroiled in a feud of some sort with highly unsavory characters. Such feuds, Slade had learned from experience, usually meant association. Hurst's gratitude to him the night of the fight in the saloon had been warmly expressed, but Slade recalled that he showed not the least surprise that somebody should try to drive a knife in his back. Which intimated that Hurst knew exactly what it was all about. Slade shook his head and went back to work.

Great progress had been made. The breakwaters were nearing completion. The end piers were firmly seated. Only the difficult center pier was not finished. The sand hogs concentrated on the chore, cursing the river, each other and themselves. Block after block of stone was engulfed by the seemingly insatiable maw of the coffer. To the north the ribbons of steel crept forward. Now the gleam of the newly laid rails could be seen. Faintly above the grumble of the swollen river sounded the chugging of the locomotives.

Slade set his transit and took sights on the breakwaters. Just as the sun sank ominously red, he signalled to the powder men and the laborers. His voice rang out —

"That should do the trick. If what you've got won't turn flood water, nothing will. Come on in!"

Shouts and waving hands answered him. The workers on the near shore trooped agilely over the broken stone to the camp. Those on the far shore negotiated the crossing via the bridge. Slade gazed with satisfaction at the current racing between the piers and not against them. He ate his dinner and then slept for three hours. The sand hogs were toiling at the center pier, but Rafferty reported that bedrock was now only a course or two away.

Morning broke gray and overcast. But an hour after daylight the workers were in a jubilant mood. Up from the center coffer poured the sand hogs, shouting and cheering.

"Bedrock!" Rafferty boomed.

Slade instantly swung into action. "Start the jacks and raise the spans," he ordered. "Masons to the front!"

The jack levers clanked and creaked. Slowly the ponderous spans rose. Slade's transit telescope swung back and forth. It took less than two hours to raise the spans to the required height.

"I wouldn't have believed it possible to do

137

the chore in so short a time," he told Rafferty. "Those boys are sure on the job."

"They wouldn't let you down, sir, if Hell froze over and pigs walked across on the ice," the grizzled foreman declared.

And then still another message came from Jaggers Dunn:

"Raining very hard just north of Carlsbad."

And Carlsbad was little more than fifty miles from the site of the bridge.

But now the graders from the railhead were busy preparing the approaches to the bridge, and right behind them with thudding mauls came the track layers.

Rutledge rode down from the railhead. "How goes it?" he asked.

"We'll be ready for you when you get here," Slade told the engineer. "You can join your steel with the rails on the bridge."

Rutledge gazed at the swollen river. "Looks bad," he commented.

"Yes, and it'll get worse, but I believe we've got it whipped," Slade replied. "All we've really got to worry about now is a flash flood, but it wouldn't surprise me a bit if we get that. I predict it'll be raining here within an hour."

138

Slade was right. It was raining within the hour, raining hard; but the work never slackened for a moment. The stone blocks swung in the derrick slings. The trowels of the masons sloshed and scraped. Barrow loads of cement poured down. The blocks were set in place, the joints fitted with the utmost nicety.

The river was rising fast, but faster still rose the piers. Slade had rodmen stationed at each pier. He took sight after sight, figured calculations on soaked paper, estimated, revised his estimates, arrived at definite conclusions.

Again the night, pitch black, but flares and bonfires made the scene bright as day. Brighter, in fact, than the gray and rain streaked dawn that broke at last. Slade, who hadn't had a wink of sleep, heaved a sigh of relief as he viewed what had been accomplished during the night.

"We're going to do it," he told Cassidy. "Tell the boys we don't want those track layers to beat us to it and have to wait."

Cassidy relayed the message to the workers and the tempo of activity increased even a little more.

Slade noted that the graders and steel men were busy putting down a short siding, and as he gazed he saw a big locomotive boom-

139

ing down from the northeast and drawing a single coach. He chuckled. Jaggers Dunn himself was coming to watch the finish. A little later the private coach eased cautiously onto the newly laid siding and the stocky figure of the general manager strode through the rain.

"Regular deluge south of Carlsbad," he told Slade. "Yes, a regular cloudburst."

"Guess we're going to catch it," Slade replied, "but I think we'll be ready." He set the tripod of his transit firmly, swung the telescope around. With the greatest care he took his sights. An hour later he again took sights. His voice rang out —

"That does it! Lower away!"

The masons came swarming onto the span. The jack handles began their steady clanking.

"We've got to get the weight of the spans on that green masonry," Slade told Dunn. "Otherwise it won't withstand the water that's liable to come down any time now."

Lowering the spans was a slow and tedious job and had to be done with the utmost precision. Slade was everywhere, ordering, advising. Finally he took up his post on the center pier with Rafferty and watched the massive beams of the spans settle down, their progress hardly perceptible to the naked eye. He glanced down at the water surging and frothing against the pier, gazed upstream to where the current stormed against the breakwaters.

Another hour of toil and suspense and the spans were all but touching the piers. Slade raised his head to listen. The swollen Pecos had taken to itself a new sound. A high-pitched whine threaded through its mutter and grumble, and now the water was rising higher by the minute.

"It's coming," Slade told Rafferty. "We're going to get a flash flood sure as blazes!"

Behind him sounded a long-drawn cry — *"Bedrock!"*

"And not a minute too soon!" Slade shouted above the bellow of the river. "Listen!"

From the canyon to the north came a mighty rumbling that rose and rose.

On the piers, brawny arms tightened the nuts on the great bolts imbedded in the masonry, the steel men working with frantic speed. Up came the jacks, the jackmen swarming after them. Scant minutes later the workers on the piers climbed to the top of the span and raced for safety, Slade last of all.

The mighty rumbling had loudened until it quivered the air like the diapson of hammered steel. Out of the canyon burst a wall of water, tossing, raving, rushing forward with racehorse speed. It struck the massive breakwaters with a voice of thunder, hurled showers of spray scores of feet in the air. Seething, whirling, it raged against the barriers of stone. With a wild yell, big Rafferty paused long enough to throw his hat straight at the rushing flood.

"Do your domdest!" he howled. "You're licked, ye spalpeen, you're licked."

Straight for the bridge stormed the diverted torrent — straight between the piers. The coffer dams went to pieces like matchwood. The clusters of piling that had supported the jacks, reeled, swayed, and were gone. The tossing water rose to within less than two feet of the bottom of the spans.

But the bridge, its piers anchored on the eternal rock, stood firm!

Cheer after cheer arose. The locomotive whistle shrieked and shrieked. The powder men set off charges of dynamite. Slade turned to Jaggers Dunn.

"Well, sir," he said, "I guess that's about all."

TWELVE

An hour later, to the accompaniment of more cheers, the G.M.'s private car rolled onto the bridge and came to a halt over the center span. Heedless of the defeated Pecos, which muttered angry but watery curses beneath them, Slade and General Manager Dunn enjoyed an excellent dinner together. After a while, Dunn shoved a box of long, smooth Havanas across to Slade and helped himself to one.

"Well," he said, blowing out a cloud of smoke, "well, I got the lowdown on your Cattleman's Exchange Bank. It was a hard chore of digging through a maze of interlocking directorates, but my lawyers finally hit paydirt. The syndicate that bought the bank is controlled by the holding company which also controls the M. K. Railroad. That bank is now part of their financial structure."

Slade smoked in silence for several minutes, digesting this bit of information.

"As usual," he said at length, "whenever there's trouble of any kind in a section where it runs, I can rely on finding your darn railroad mixed up in it in some way or other. I never knew it to fail. Now I wonder why did the M. K. want that small cowtown bank?"

"They own quite a few of 'em," Dunn remarked.

"Doubtless," Slade agreed, "but I'll wager that in this instance there is some sort of financial shenanigan in the making. Just what I haven't the slightest notion, at the moment, but I *have* a notion it will prove interesting."

"Very likely you are right, you usually are," grunted Jaggers. He hauled a slip of paper from his pocket and tossed it across the table.

"I'm not trying to pay you for what you did, that isn't possible," he said. "That's just a small token of my appreciation, and I hope you'll accept it in the spirit in which it is given. It will help you to starve with the Rangers a while longer, instead of taking a paying job with the road. When are you going to do it, Walt?"

"Sooner or later, I suppose," Slade replied. "Right now I feel that I'm doing a little good with the Rangers, and getting a chance now and then to advantage deserving people who are in need of a helping hand."

Jaggers Dunn looked at him with a curious expression. In that look was the tribute, unconscious, perhaps, of the man whose life has been spent mostly in the conquest of material things to the man who has the audacity, insensate though it seems, to fling these to the winds in his search for ideals.

"I hope you'll make it sooner, before something happens to you," he said.

Slade nodded. He studied the check a moment, which was for no small amount, hesitated, glanced at Dunn, and slipped it in his pocket.

"Thank you, sir," he said.

The rain had ceased and the sun was shining brightly the following morning. Slade made a last tour of inspection and, satisfied that everything was as it should be, he shook hands with all the workers and rode for Benton.

"See you payday," Rafferty shouted after him. "We aim to have a high old time and you got to be with us or we'll all feel mighty bad."

"I'll try to be," Slade promised, and meant it. Once again he was strictly a Ranger and he felt that payday in Benton might possibly be productive of needed results.

When he reached Benton he stabled his horse and repaired to the Queen High for a cup of coffee and a snack. He was giving his order to a waiter when two men entered and made their way to the bar. Slade instantly recognized the smaller as Jason Gaunt, the new manager of the Muerto bank. His companion was tall and broad-shouldered, with a thin-lipped mouth that did not seem to move when he spoke. He had dark, watchful eyes that glinted in the shadow of his hatbrim. His clean-shaven face was lean and tanned. Slade sensed something vaguely familiar about his build, his eyes and his prominent nose.

"Those two men who just came in," he remarked to the waiter. "Do you happen to know the taller one?"

"Why, yes," the waiter replied. "That's Mr. Parks Trimble, the real estate man. He drops in frequently; real friendly with the boss, Richmond Hurst, you know. Mr. Hurst stores papers and money in Mr. Trimble's safe; I've packed things there for him more than once. Mr. Trimble is a fine man and a good spender. The other feller has been in here with him a couple of times. I don't know who he is. Anything else with the coffee, sir?"

"No, that will be all, and thank you," Slade replied.

While waiting to be served, Slade studied the pair at the bar, still impressed by the feeling that he had seen the tall man before, though where and in what connection he hadn't the slightest notion. What was Gaunt, the bank manager, doing in his company, he wondered idly?

The answer to that, however, was fairly obvious. Doubtless Trimble, in the course of his real estate manipulations, had extensive dealings with the bank. He continued to study Trimble, baffled by the elusive illusion, if it was illusion, of familiarity, and wracked his brains in an endeavor to recall where and under what circumstances he might have seen the man, to no avail.

"Seems of late I'm all the time seeing somebody or something that reminds me of somebody or something," he grumbled to himself. The thing suddenly called to mind, he drew the plat of the cadastral survey he took from the person of the dead drygulcher he was convinced had been none other than Lafe Whittaker, the missing engineer who built the bridge across the Pecos. Spreading the plat on the table, he studied it intently. Abruptly his eyes glowed.

"Well, I've got this one spotted, anyhow,"

he told the salt shaker. "It's a survey of that peculiarly shaped mesa on John Trout's holding. No doubt about it. The same hourglass shape, with the north bulb larger than the south one. The same directional notations. The same extent measurements, checking with what Trout said of the mesa. But why in blazes would Whittaker, or anybody else, make such an accurate survey of that shove-dup hunk of rock? Oh, the devil. Find the answer to one question and immediately another pops up!" He seized the unresponsive shaker and sprinkled his meat with the contents.

Richmond Hurst entered a few minutes later. He waved to Slade, paused at the bar to shake hands and chat cordially with Trimble and Gaunt. His face grew animated as he talked. Several times Gaunt and Trimble glanced in Slade's direction. Finally the saloonkeeper led his companions across the room to Slade's table.

"Slade," said Hurst, "I believe you've met Mr. Gaunt, but I want you to know Mr. Parks Trimble, the real estate man."

Trimble shook hands with a firm grip, his keen, dark eyes took Slade in from head to foot.

"I am honored, Mr. Slade," he said. "I was greatly impressed by your recent exploit. We were all a bit jittery over the outcome. I don't hesitate to predict that the C. & P. losing the race to the coast would have an adverse effect on this section."

Slade did not argue that point. Jaggers Dunn was noted for his interest in the development of communities through which his road ran, and was always ready to lend a helping hand where one was needed. So much could not be said for the M. K., to put it mildly. The M. K. motto was, "All the traffic will bear."

Again Slade experienced the vague, fleeting impression that he had seen Trimble somewhere before. Oh, well, perhaps it was just on the streets of Benton. Trimble was a man to attract one's attention.

After a few minutes' pleasant but inconsequential conversation, Gaunt and Trimble went back to the bar. Shortly afterward they left the saloon.

Hurst sauntered over and dropped into a chair opposite Slade.

"Everybody's singing your praises," he said. "I followed your progress with great interest myself. Not only because of a personal interest in yourself, but because of what you might call an inherited interest in railroads."

"How is that?" Slade asked.

"My father was a railroad engineer, later a division superintendent on the Santa Fe," Hurst explained. "I worked in the shops and roundhouses some myself, at Topeka. Rather liked it. Had itchy feet, though, and wandered west. Worked for a few spreads and bummed around generally. Saw there was money in the saloon business and when Dad passed on and left me some, I got into the business myself, following construction towns like this one and cashing in before the construction camps moved on. A man can make a nice profit during the few months such a town exists."

"You are conversant with railroad affairs, then," Slade observed.

"Enough so to read the signs a-right," Hurst replied with a quick smile. "Well, I've got to go and check stock. Be a big night the last of the week — payday for the railroaders, and for most of the neighborhood ranches. Everybody will be in town."

After Hurst departed, Slade sat smoking thoughtfully. Taken at face value, what Hurst had just told him explained his setting up a permanent establishment in Muerto. Not hard for him to guess that Muerto, not Benton, would be Division and Junction. He wondered if Parks Trimble, who also undoubtedly knew Benton had

150

never been intended for Division, could offer as simple an explanation. Slade did not think so. It appeared that Trimble knew the truth long before construction headquarters were set up at Benton. How did he acquire the closely guarded information? Slade didn't know, and wished he did.

Thirteen

Early the following morning, Walt Slade rode out of Benton, headed west. At Bleached Bones Crossing he forded the Pecos, now a much subdued river, perhaps remembering its recent defeat at the hands of this tall biped with the black hair and gray eyes, although probably a more prosaic explanation would be the ceasing of the rains to the north.

Negotiating the crossing without difficulty, Slade rode steadily till he reached the Lazy K ranchhouse. Old John Trout was sitting on the veranda and when he recognized his visitor let out a bellow of greeting.

"Was beginning to wonder if you'd forgotten us," he said, shaking hands with vigor. "Verna! we've got company!"

Verna appeared in the doorway, smiling. Slade thought she looked even more charming than the last time he saw her.

"Let's eat," said Trout. "Company coming

152

always makes me hungry."

After they finished eating, Trout had to hear all about the conquest of the Pecos. He listened with interest to Slade's terse account.

"Not often that darned old river takes a larrupin'," he said. "Sometimes it acts as if it were alive."

"It sure looked that way when the flash flood roared down on the bridge," Slade agreed soberly. "One little miscalculation at the breakwaters and we would have had trouble. How are things going with you, sir?"

"Oh, we're jogging along," Trout replied. "Money is mighty tight, but now I've got that infernal mortgage off my neck, we'll make out, I hope."

Slade glanced out the window at the sun. "It isn't late," he said to Verna. "How'd you like to take a ride? I've looked at mud and water so much of late, a cow's tail will appear plumb beautiful by contrast."

"I'd love it," she answered. "I'll have one of the wranlers get my horse while I change to something more suitable for riding. This skirt is short and rather tight. I've a notion it would do considerable climbing."

"Never mind changing it," Slade instantly returned. Verna giggled and trotted up the stairs.

Old John chuckled as he watched them ride away. "The gal's lucky," he said to Ed Block. "Two fine young fellers, Slade and Richmond Hurst, following her around."

"Hurst will follow, but Slade will lead," the range boss replied sententiously. "Slade will be riding off after a while, but I predict Hurst will be tagging along after her for a long, long time."

"I've a notion she could do worse," said old John. "Hurst strikes me as being an up and coming young feller."

Slade deftly steered the course to the southwest; he wanted to have another look at the peculiarly shaped mesa and try and figure out why the blazes anybody would want to make a survey of the darn thing.

"I've been up there," Verna said as they drew near the strange plateau. "It's beautiful and peaceful. Those little trees grow so close together, thousands and thousands of them, their trunks straight as arrows, with here and there a gnarled old patriarch shooting up I don't know how high and spreading its branches over them like a hen spreads her wings over chicks."

"How'd you get up?" Slade asked.

"There's a place not far to the south where it can be climbed, on foot," she replied. "No horse could make it. Like for

154

me to show you?"

"I would," Slade answered. "Suppose we climb it together?"

They followed the line of the bluffs, and when they reached the spot Verna mentioned Slade recognized it as the "waist" of the "hourglass" as shown on the plat he carried in his pocket, where the mesa was only about three miles in width.

On closer inspection, the explanation of the peculiar formation was obvious, a softer strata of rock than that which flanked the waist on either side, scored out by erosion in the course of untold ages.

The ascent was arduous but not particularly dangerous and after a good deal of scrambling they reached the summit, Slade assisting the girl the last hundred feet or so. He carried her the final dozen yards, for she was breathless, her cheeks flushed, her red lips parted. As he set her on her feet he leaned over and kissed her.

"That's one *he* won't get," he said laughingly.

"He?" she asked, her blue eyes all innocence. "Oh, well, I guess he won't miss one, or even two, for that matter."

Slade accepted the obvious invitation, after which they laughed together and set out to explore the wooded expanse.

155

The growth was principally small stuff, with trunks averaging ten or twelve inches in diameter. But there was a fair sprinkling of splendid trees running up to fully a hundred and fifty feet in height.

As they roved about the groves, they came upon signs of recent visitors to the plateau. Several times they discovered what had undoubtedly been camping sites, with blackened stones to indicate fires.

"Looks like somebody has been having picnics up here," Verna observed.

"Could be," Slade replied. Somebody or somebodies had spent considerable time on the crest, but he did not think picnicking was the answer.

After they had descended and mounted their horses, Slade paused to gazed at the wooded crest. Suddenly his hand tightened on the bridle till his knuckles showed white.

"Of all the stupid jackasses!" he bitterly castigated himself, under his breath. "You really touch the limit! You enlarge my view of the possible! Mental inertia! Cerebral paresis! Wonderful! Right under your nose all the time, and you never saw it till now!"

"What did you say?" Verna asked.

"Just humming," he evaded. "Guess we'd better head for home if we don't want to spend the night out here."

"Well?"

"I don't thing even *he* would condone that," Slade smiled. "And quite likely your father would escort us to town in the morning, with a shotgun."

"Worse things could happen, but they won't," she said. "Let's go!"

She sent her horse scudding across the prairie. Shadow snorted angrily at such impudence, and proceeded to draw abreast of the flying sorrel without difficulty.

Slade was in a complacent mood, although thoroughly disgusted with himself for his own slowness of perception, as they rode home through the soft beauty of the dusk. At long last things were tieing up. The following morning he announced his intention of riding to Benton.

"I have a business matter to take up with Mr. Dunn, and I want to be in town for the payday celebration," he explained to Trout.

"Think I'll ride in tomorrow myself," the rancher replied. "I aint so old but I still enjoy a bust, and of course, the boys will want to go."

"That will be fine," Slade said. "I'll meet you tomorrow afternoon, at the Queen High."

When he reached Benton, Slade at once repaired to General Manager Dunn's private car.

"Sit down and have a cigar," invited the railroad magnate. "Sam, break out a bottle. What's on your mind, son? You look like a cat that has just lapped up a saucer of cream and sees the door of the canary's cage open."

"Everything considered, I feel sort of that way," Slade admitted. "I gather, sir, that you have to haul all your crossties and other timber quite a distance?"

"You're right," growled Dunn. "It costs us a pretty penny and makes for irritating delay. Why?"

Slade countered with a question of his own. "Suppose, sir," he said, "suppose you could get a million prime live oak ties right here in this section, would you buy them?"

"Would I buy them!" snorted Dunn. "They could well mean winning the race to the coast. Would I buy them! I'd buy the moon, too, if it was solid gold and I could get it."

"Well, I can't answer for the moon, but I can answer for the ties," Slade said. He explained in detail the mesa and the enormous growth of live oaks on its summit.

"All small stuff that will require a minimum of trimming and shaping," he concluded. "With an addition of valuable large

158

timber that I imagine you can use."

"But how the devil will you get them down?" Dunn demanded. "As I understand you, it would be practically impossible to build a logging road to the crest, and you can't tumble logs over a two-hundred-foot cliff and expect them to be any good after they hit the bottom."

"Ever hear of an overhead conveyor system?" Slade asked. The General Manager's eyes glowed. "Of course," he replied. "I've seen them bringing ore down from the hills in big iron buckets attached to pulleys running on overhead cables stretched between towers."

"Substitute grippers with automatic trips for the buckets and you can bring the logs down from the crest without scratching the bark," Slade said.

Jaggers Dunn hammered his desk with a big fist. "By George! you've hit it!" he exclaimed.

"And I suppose you can expedite acquiring and delivering the necessary machinery?" Slade asked.

"Of course," Dunn replied. "Steel being laid beyond the bridge will make the chore much less complicated. And I'll bring in a gang of loggers to fell the trees. You're sure Trout will sell?"

"Of course," Slade answered. "Why shouldn't he? He needs money, and he's got a fortune up top those cliffs, just waiting to be gathered in. He's coming to town tomorrow for the payday celebration. I'll bring him here and you can talk business."

"Slade," Dunn said, "as I remarked once before, you're a life-saver if there ever was one. You'll superintend the logging?"

"Yes," Slade agreed. "As I said before, I can always count on your railroad being in the middle of anything off color going on in a section, innocently, of course, but right there. This is no exception. I'm beginning to see my way clear to doing what I was sent here to do."

"Sam," said General Manager Dunn, "break out another bottle."

The dawn was breaking in flaming splendor when Slade awoke after a good night's rest. The east was scarlet and gold and pulsing crimson, the rangeland myriad shades of green spangled with fiery gems of dew that a gentle wind shook down in showers of glittering light. In the darkling west a single great star still glowed and trembled, paled from gold to silver, dwindled to a steely needle-point and vanished as the frosted ebony of the sky changed to the deepest

160

blue. Coruscating spears, flung upward from the eastern horizon, stabbed the zenith with their glowing lance heads, widened, deepened, spread in gleaming bands of radiance until the whole mighty arch was drenched with brilliance and the earth below was a sea of molten bronze.

A lance of light fell downward, clove the shadows and shot upward an answering gleam from the railroad's steel. As if, Slade thought, the star of empire had risen from the blackness to light the way for its marching legions that were to follow.

Benton lay without sound or motion in its setting of jade and emerald, its unslightly shacks and 'dobes and its gaunt shop and roundhouse mellowed and softened in the golden light, its tents flashing white like snow. After that first glad whisper of the dawn wind, the morning was so still and quiet that no leaf trembled, no grass blade bent, no gossamer quivered its frosty mist of pearl and amethyst. The smoke plume that always hung over the construction town was stained with a dye of crushed violets, its edges drenched with rose. The distant Pecos was a torrent of royal purple flecked with garnet and ruby as the light strengthened.

But gradually a murmur began in the

161

silent town, a murmur that rose to a hum punctuated by a banging of shutters and a creaking of opening doors. Benton was awakening to the wildest day and night it had yet known. The sun rose on a scene of activity and preparation.

A train boomed in from the west, its long line of flat cars black with men from the camps at the railhead. Another followed, and still another. The gray of the Pecos Trail was flecked with dots which resolved to hurrying horsemen, all headed for Benton. They bulged into town, pulled their horses to a slithering halt before the long hitchracks that fronted every saloon. Cowhands rode in from the west, the north and the south. And sprinkled among the knots of carefree punchers, Slade noted, were other riders, quiet watchful riders with hard faces and all-seeing eyes. These last kept mostly to themselves and did not mingle with the gaily chattering waddies, but missed nothing of what went on around them.

Soon the dust of the main street that was the Pecos Trail was churned to smoldering clouds, its particles glinting golden in the strengthening sunlight. The board sidewalks dinned to the pound of boot-heels, a babble of talk wafted from the open doors of saloons, shops, and gambling halls. Benton was gathering itself together, quickening, stirring with lusty life.

Slade's spirit was uplifted as he walked in a world all glorious with morning, vigorous and confident in his youth and strength. But his face grew grim as he reflected on what was to come, on what the day and the night would bring forth. This would be no ordinary payday celebration. It would be the wildest and very likely the blackest and deadliest Benton would ever know.

Hundreds of construction workers gathered in the railroad yards, a crowd that was constantly augmented by new arrivals. A holiday spirit pervaded the throng. Snatches of song were carolled in lusty fashion with little regard for time or tune. There was animated conversation as men talked excitedly of what they intended to do with the gold that soon would be dropped into their hands from the paycar windows — gold stained with the sweat of bitter toil, too often crusted with dried blood and darkened with the black shadow of tragedy.

But what did all that matter! Life was cheap, and fleeting. Life was to be enjoyed to the full while it still pulsed and quickened. There might be bitter dregs in the cup, but the wine was good! Drink deep! Yesterday and its sufferings are a forgotten

163

shadow. Tomorrow a thing unborn, unpredictable, unworthy of serious consideration because it might never happen.

Behind them the shack town waited, crouched like a monster eager to gorge. Bartenders stood expectantly behind the bars. The cold-eyed, iron-nerved card dealers sat at their green-clothed tables, awaiting the golden harvest. Orchestras tuned up. The dance-floors were shining with wax. The roulette wheels gleamed and glittered with a mocking allure. The dance-floor girls flaunted their short skirts and their silks and satins, peering eagerly with too-bright eyes toward the yawning doorways. From the lunch counters floated appetizing aromas of cooking food and steaming coffee. Benton was ready and waiting.

Far to the east, where the shining rails drew together, seemingly, appeared a crawling bug that swiftly grew in size. A low humming of the rails heralded its coming. It grew more, and still more, resolved into a big locomotive drawing a single coach. A mutter quivered the air, swelled to a staccato rumble. Into the yards thundered the paycar train, rising safety valve roaring, the blower booming in the stack as it swirled the cloud of black smoke streaked with steam high in the crystal air. The engine swerved, air gushed through the port and with a clang and clatter of brake-rigging and a screaming of shoes on the tires, the pay-car came to a halt on a siding. The doors were flung open, the brass-grilled windows banged up and a steady stream of men began filing through one end of the car and out the other.

As if in sympathy with the spirit that pervaded the crowd, the day which had dawned so quietly grew boisterous. A rising wind flung the white dust of the streets into the air. It streaked the clothes of the throng, swirled in through open doors and windows. But nobody heeded it any more than they heeded the blaze of the mounting sun. The cool interiors of the buildings yawned to receive the celebrating workers, cowboys, and riders from the hills who had come to town to take their share of the general hell-raising.

Quickly the bars were lined. The clink of bottle necks on glass rims joined the tumult of song and talk. The idle roulette wheels began to whir and click. The dealers shuffled their cards. The orchestras blared forth music, or what passed for it. Benton was fully awake now, stretching herself, beginning with a purr that would, before the sun sank in glory behind the western hills, rise to a savage howl to affright the shuddering stars.

Payday! The last payday before the bitter fight to conquer the wild and dangerous terrain between the Pecos and Muerto, town with an ominous name. Make it a good one! Plenty of us won't be around to celebrate the next one! Who the devil knows who will and who won't! Don't take any chances on missing something! Maybe your number is up. Take your fill before the dark "croupier" yells and you see you're on the black when you played the red!

FOURTEEN

Slade dropped in for a chat with Jaggers Dunn, who was sitting in his private car gazing out the window at the turbulent scene.

"It's going to be a lulu," said Dunn. "The last payday for Benton. The next one will be at Muerto. Queer sounding name for a town."

" 'The dead'," nodded Slade. "Loosely translated, it means 'Dead Man'."

"Well, I've a notion there's going to be a resurrection there before long," Dunn remarked dryly. "Let's see, your logging operations will be only a few miles from Muerto, right? Which means another bunch of salty hombres to help whoop things up. Loggers are bad as railroad builders. I was thinking of something funny. There was a construction town on the Union Pacific when they were building that line, way back in the Sixties. It was named Benton, and was a snorter for fair."

167

"Let's hope the similarity of names isn't prophetic," Slade smiled.

"You can hope, but I wager you'll change your mind before the night is over," Dunn predicted. "This is going to be one to remember. Oh, well, the West was, and is, built on whiskey, cards and women. Wherever there's progress you'll find all three. Guess it's been that way since the beginning. According to the Scriptures, it was a woman stated things moving in the first place. Whiskey and cards, or their equivalents, came a bit later to keep the ball rolling. You say Trout will be in this afternoon?"

"He should make it right after noon," Slade replied.

"I'll be waiting to talk business," said the G.M. "Bring him around."

Slade promised to do so and went out to look things over. He had a growing feeling that Jaggers Dunn would prove himself no mean prophet. To all appearances, Benton was due to stage a shindig that would be talked about when the C. & P. was double-tracked from coast to coast. More and more horsemen were riding in, often with their mounts in a lather of sweat, their clothes thickly powdered with the dust of long and hard traveling. Evidently the more distant spreads had also paid off so that their hands

168

could join the other revellers in Benton.

John Trout put in an appearance shortly after noon and met Slade in the Queen High. They found a vacant table in a corner, sat down and ordered drinks. A perspiring waiter with whom Slade had talked at times brought them quickly.

"Mr. Hurst said everything is on the house," he chuckled. "Please don't argue with him, he's in a bad enough temper already. Swears he never wants to see another payday. And look at Algy Ragnall, the floor manager. See how he's batting his hands together? That means busted heads for some folks. Algy is a teetotaller, never touches a drop, but he gets drunker on excitement than he would on red-eye."

Slade chuckled as he gazed at the huge dwarf. Ragnall's brown eyes were snapping and he looked altogether joyous.

"How's things going, son?" Trout asked as he raised his glass.

"Fine as frog's hair," Slade replied. "I've got something to tell you."

"Shoot," said old John, looking expectant.

A little later, John Trout was the most astonished rancher west of the Pecos.

"Son, I just can't believe it," he said. "I never figured those darn trees to be worth a hoot."

"They're worth a fortune," Slade replied. "You'll be on easy street when the chore is finished."

"So will you," Trout declared. "You're in on this, son."

Slade shook his head in a way that Trout knew was final. "Many thanks, sir," he said, "but I've a few pesos laid away against a rainy day, and I don't need much in my line of — work."

Old John looked very disappointed. "It'll take money to get things started," he remarked.

"Yes, it will," Slade agreed. "I'm sure Mr. Dunn would advance you the money you need, but —" He hesitated, offered a suggestion, hoping to heaven he wasn't making a mistake.

"But why don't you go to Hurst for the money? That would keep everything in your hands. I'm sure he has it, and I'm just as sure he'd let you have it."

"That's a notion," said Trout. "I'll do more, I'll take him in with me on the deal. That oughta help keep him in the section. I'd hate to have my gal packing off someplace where I wouldn't get to see her often."

"There is one more thing I feel it my duty to mention," Slade said. "If you approached the M. K., they would bid against the C. &

P. for the ties, and shoot the price up."

Trout tugged his mustache reflectively. "What about this feller Dunn?" he asked.

"A square man, and my friend," Slade answered.

Old John polished off his glass with gusto. "Guess we don't need to bother with the M. K.," he said. "I like to deal with square men. We'll go see Dunn after we've had a couple more drinks."

At that moment two men entered and found a spot where they could get drinks by reaching over the heads of those lining the bar. One was of medium build with a grubby, stupid looking face. The other was tall, broad-shouldered, with a heavy growth of black beard reaching almost to his cheek bones. His hat was drawn low over his eyes.

Slade gazed at him, and once again he was struck by the limpness of the beard, which, though luxuriant, hung down in a discouraged manner. Suddenly he uttered a sharp exclamation, under his breath.

"John," he said, "don't turn around and don't make it obvious, but take a look at those two fellows standing just this side of the bar, the tall one and a short one."

Trout eased in his chair a little and surveyed the pair from the corners of his eyes.

"Well, I'll be hanged!" he muttered. "It's

171

those two hellions who were giving us such a once-over the night you packed the money to the ranch. The little one was with them that night, the sidewinder you shot off the bluff."

"Do you recognize the tall one?" Slade asked softly.

"Can't say as I ever saw him before, except that night," Trout replied. "Do you?"

"Yes," Slade answered. "He's Parks Trimble, the real estate man. I've been wondering who the devil it was Trimble reminded me of. It was himself, wearing a false beard. I'm sure that beard is false from the limp way it hangs. A false beard never bristles."

"But what in blazes is he doing sashayin' around in such a get-up?" sputtered Trout.

"I imagine he doesn't want to be recognized in the company of certain folks," Slade said. "Pretty good disguise, all right. Rough rangeland clothes instead of a business suit, and the beard isn't bad. Chances are hardly anybody would spot it as being false. And with his hat-brim pulled down low, he doesn't look much like Trimble as people hereabouts know him. This is getting interesting. I wonder what the deuce is in the wind tonight?"

"I don't know, but I do know a feller who

goes around covering up ain't to be trusted." Trout declared. "Especially when he hangs out with drygulching horned toads like the one that tried to do for us down there by the mesa. Sheriff Dobson is in town, swearin' in special deputies. Think we'd better tell him about it?"

"No, not yet," Slade replied. "And, John, I'd take it as a favor if you'd keep what I told you under your hat till I give the word."

"Don't worry, I'll keep a tight latigo on my jaw," Trout instantly agreed. "Don't know what you've got going in your think tank, but whatever it is, I know it's okay."

Slade nodded, and sat silent, endeavoring to properly evaluate what he had just learned and fit it in with what he already knew. Although all the threads were not yet in his hands, the pattern was beginning to take shape. When, a little later, Trimble and his companion left the saloon, he turned to Trout.

"Suppose we go have a talk with Mr. Dunn," he suggested.

The interview with the general manager was satisfactory to all concerned. Dunn named a price per tie that Slade estimated would give old John a fair profit.

"I'll have the papers drawn up and sent to you without delay, Mr. Trout," Jaggers said.

"Slade can make a list of what is needed and start things moving. You should be able to set up in business within a week or so. If you have trouble raising the money you'll want, come and see me. I agree with Slade that it's always best to have local capital finance such projects, if possible, but if you meet with difficulties, don't hesitate to come to me.

"I'm just as anxious to buy those ties as you are to sell them," he added with a quick smile. "Sam! break out a bottle!"

As the lovely blue dusk began to sift down from the hills, the growing howl of Benton welled to a bellow. The red-eye men had been drinking all day was beginning to get in its licks. The clean tang of sawdust on the saloon floors was befouled with the reek of spilled whiskey, and already, in more than one place, by the raw and piercing smell of spilled blood. There had been fights during the day, but none of a serious nature, a shooting or two that didn't amount to much and were largely the result of exuberant spirits, a number of ruckuses that were productive of black eyes and busted noses which were forgotten almost as quickly as the combatants were pulled apart.

But now, as the night descended, nerves were getting raw, tempers were roughened.

174

Men began walking stiff-backed and truculent, their hands close to the weapons that swung at their belts. Bartenders, dealers and floor men became more alert. The special deputies braced themselves for trouble.

It was not long in coming. In the Bear Cat saloon, guns suddenly flamed. When the smoke had cleared away, two men lay dead on the sawdust and another was bleeding profusely from a bullet-smashed shoulder. A Mexican leaned across a poker table, steel flashing in his hand. Before he could rip the throat of the man opposite him, a dealer flipped a short-barrelled derringer from his sleeve and smashed the hand that held the knife. The Mexican dropped his steel with a yowl of pain. His adversary, who had instantly "reached," slid his Colt back into its holster as he stared into the black muzzle of the dealer's sleeve gun. The dealer flipped the wicked little weapon back into his sleeve and shuffled the deck as calmly as if nothing had happened. The glowering Mexican peered at his hole card, clumsily fingering his chips with his left hand. The man he had tried to knife bet two blues and, a moment later, raked in the pot. The Mexican won the next one and the pair grinned across the table at each other, their differences forgotten in the excitement of good hands of cards.

Slade watched the tremendous crowd in Richmond Hurst's Queen High for a while, his eyes thoughtful. He hunted up Sheriff Ad Dobson and had a little talk with him.

"A good idea," Dobson agreed to what Slade suggested. "I wouldn't want anything to happen to that private car. I've a notion Dunn can take care of himself, but it's best not to take chances; I'll do what you say. You'll speak to Hurst?"

"Yes, I'll see him," Slade promised. He returned to the Queen High and contacted Hurst, who appeared in a very bad temper indeed.

"What are you doing with the money you've taken in today?" Slade asked. "It must be a small fortune."

"I've got it stashed away in my desk in the back room, with a floor man standing guard over it with a shotgun," Hurst replied. "A little later I'll send it to Trimble's office and he'll put it in his strongbox."

"Don't," Slade said. Hurst stared at him.

"Don't," Slade repeated. "Some strange things may happen in this town tonight. Send it over to Mr. Dunn's private car and he'll stow it in his big safe. There are two railroad policemen and three special deputies guarding that car. And don't let anybody see you pass it to your messenger."

Hurst looked a bit bewildered, but he nodded his head. "Okay, if you say so," he acceded. "Give me fifteen minutes and I'll have it on its way with a man I can trust."

"I'll arrange matters with Mr. Dunn," Slade promised, and left the saloon.

As Slade neared the private car, Deputy Mark Sullivan and one of his specials stepped from the shadows.

"Hello, Slade," said Sullivan, recognizing El Halcon. "Going in to see Mr. Dunn?"

"That's right," Slade replied, "and listen, Mark." He spoke a few words in a low tone.

"Okay," said the deputy. "We'll pass him in. A good notion, I think. No telling what will happen in this seven-devil town tonight."

Slade found Jaggers Dunn sitting at his desk, a glass in front of him, contemplatively smoking a big cigar. He waved a greeting.

"Sure I'll take care of it for him," he agreed, after Slade had stated his errand. "He's the fellow Trout is going to get his money from, isn't he? We wouldn't want anything to happen to that money. Tell him to keep it coming; I'll be up all night, anyhow. Sam! break out a bottle."

Shortly after Hurst's messenger had arrived and departed, Slade left the private car and wandered around the roaring town for a while. He dropped in at the Bear Cat, the Red Front, the Ace-Full, and other places. All were doing a roaring business, and in all there had been trouble. Not yet midnight and Benton was really beginning to howl. Slade went back to the Queen High and joined Richmond Hurst at the end of the bar.

"Just sent another pokeful over to Dunn," the saloon-keeper said in a low voice. "I'm feeling good about that money, it could represent a heavy loss. Feeling better than some of the other boys, I've a notion, including the Bear Cat and the Ace-Full. They've been sending their dinero to Trimble. That old strongbox of his must be loaded."

Slade's eyes narrowed. "Good Lord! why didn't I think of that!" he muttered to himself. Aloud he said, "Where's Trimble's office located?"

"Right around the next corner to the west, a few doors down on the side street," said Hurst. "Excuse me! Looks like a row building up at the faro bank." He hurried away to restore order. Slade left the saloon and walked swiftly to the corner and turned down a quiet side street that was poorly lighted by lanterns hanging on poles. He had taken only a few steps when from directly ahead came a muffled boom. Slade raced forward and a moment later saw Trimble's name, and "Real Estate," lettered on a dimly lighted window. His nostrils stung with the acrid tang of dynamite smoke.

The door of the office was closed. Slade hit it with his shoulder backed by two hundred pounds of bone and muscle. The door flew open with a crash. Slade took in the room in a single swift glance.

Lying in a far corner, bound and gagged, was Parks Trimble. Two ruptured sandbags spilled their contents on the floor. The door of a small iron safe stood open. Beside it knelt two masked men who were transferring its contents to canvas sacks. They leaped erect with yelps of alarm.

"Elevate!" Slade shouted. "You're covered!"

Just in time he saw the gleam of shifted metal. The room rocked and thundered to the bellow of guns.

Seconds later, blood streaming down the side of his face and dripping from the fingers of his left hand, Slade lowered his smoking Colts and peered through the murk at the two figures sprawled on the floor. Regretfully, he saw that both robbers were dead and would tell no tales this side of Judgment Day. He bolstered his guns, mopped some of the blood from his bullet-grazed cheek and strode to where Trimble lay. A few strokes of his knife freed the real estate man. He pulled away the gag, which was nothing but a handkerchief bound loosely across his mouth, and helped him to a sitting position.

"You all right?" he asked.

"I — I guess so," stuttered Trimble, who seemed stupefied with astonishment. "How — how did you get here?" he added thickly.

"Was up at the corner and heard the dynamite let go," Slade replied. "Thought I'd better have a look. How'd they come to grab you?"

"Belted me over the head as I stepped out the door," Trimble muttered, rubbing his thick hair. "Dragged me back into the room and tied me up and went to work on the safe. Are — are they dead?"

"If they aren't, some jigger with a spade is going to play a mighty mean joke on them about tomorrow," Slade replied grimly. "Think you can stand up?"

"Yes, yes, I'm all right," Trimble replied, getting to his feet and glancing apprehensively at Slade's hands resting on his gun butts.

Slade stepped to where the dead men lay and stripped off their masks. One face he did not recall seeing before. The other belonged to the scrubby, middle-sized man who had been with Trimble in the Queen High a few hours earlier.

"Recognize either of them?" he asked. Trimble shook his head.

"Guess you'd better gather up that money and take it to Sheriff Dobson for safekeeping," Slade suggested.

Trimble looked dazed. "To — to the sheriff!" he repeated.

"Yes," Slade said. "I'm afraid your strongbox is out of commission."

"I guess you're right," Trimble mumbled and began stuffing the scattered gold into the canvas sacks dropped by the robbers. Over his shoulder, Slade studied the door of the safe. Its outer surface was somewhat battered and stained by the dynamite fumes, but the tumblers were shot back in their sockets and the slots which would receive them when the door was shut and locked were neither scarred nor splintered.

Outside sounded the pad of feet approaching cautiously. A moment later two of Sheriff Dobson's specials, both of whom Slade had met, loomed in the doorway with drawn guns and stared in astonishment.

"You can put away your hardware, you're a mite late," Slade told them. "Then you can escort Mr. Trimble and his money to the sheriff. Tell Dobson there are a couple of carcasses here he can arrange to dispose of."

The bewildered specials hesitated, then ducked their heads. "Okay, Mr. Slade," one said. "We heard the shooting and thought we'd better investigate. You going to stay here?"

"Tell Dobson he'll find me at the Queen High," Slade replied. He ushered them out and with a final glance around the room followed them, pulling the splintered door shut behind him.

A special marched on each side of Trimble, gun hands ready for business. Slade brought up the rear until they reached the Queen High.

"What the devil happened to you?" Richmond Hurst asked as the Ranger approached. "Your cheek's cut, and there's blood on your hand!"

Slade told him. Hurst swore incredulously. "And if it hadn't been for you they would have gotten away with it!" he exclaimed. "Say! you sure hit it off right when you had me put my money in Dunn's safe. You sure you're all right?" He glanced at Slade's bloody hand.

"Just scratches," El Halcon answered, "but I would like to wash the blood off."

"Come into the back room," said Hurst. "Water and soap and towels there. Help yourself to everything you need. I'll send in a drink; got a notion you could use one about now."

Slade examined the slight flesh wound in his arm and decided it would do without further attention for the moment. He had finished his ablutions and was sipping the drink when Sheriff Dobson entered, closing the door behind him. Slade repeated what he told Hurst.

"So the hellions caught on the saloon money was being stowed away there, eh?" the sheriff commented. "Well, I'll go look the bodies over and arrange to have them carted off."

"And while you're at it, take a good look at that safe door, and then forget what you see, for a while," Slade said.

Dobson shot him a quick look, then nodded his head. "I'll do that," he promised, adding with a grin. "Old Jim McNelty sure knows how to pick 'em!"

FIFTEEN

As the night wore on, the roar of Benton assumed a shriller note. It had been the deep-toned animal growl of lusty life unleashed. Now it was the piercing howl of nerves strained to the breaking point, of hysteria approaching the cold blackness of utter madness. The streets were full of reeling, staggering men. The dance-floors were scenes of wild abandon. The orchestras blared raucous discords. At the gaming tables men fingered stacks of gold pieces with trembling hands, cursed as they shoved them toward the cold-eyed, iron-nerved dealers, peered with bleared eyes at the cards dealt them, and cursed again.

The bars were jammed with a mass of sodden, drunken humanity. The crash of a gunshot and the scream of a stricken man were hardly heeded. The bartenders had ceased to measure drinks or draw corks. They snapped the necks of the bottles and

184

gushed the fiery liquor over the splintered glass, heedless of bleeding fingers. They forgot to make change, and nobody cared. They forgot to take pay for the drinks they poured, and nobody cared.

The spirit of utter abandon that pervaded the roaring workers infected others. The dealers grew careless, began taking the same chances as the reckless players. They forgot to win or lose with icy indifference and mingled their curses with the others. Women who had greedily clutched at gold during the early hours now cast it away with as little thought as had the men from whom they took it. Nothing had any value any more. Nothing was worth making the effort to save. The scene was atavistic, malevolent, stygian, It was a dance of elementals in Abaddon, an orgy of vampirism unleashed.

"After this, I *am* going to get out of the saloon business," Richmond Hurst declared to Slade. "Two men have been killed in here since noon, and the night isn't over yet. So this is progress! I'm beginning to wonder if it is a good thing. This is the limit!"

"It will pass," Slade said quietly, "just like a bad summer storm, with black clouds and flashing lightning and rolling thunder, and a deluge of rain that threatens to drown everything. And remember how bright and

185

green and peaceful everything is after the storm has passed away and the sun comes out again. We wouldn't appreciate the sunshine and peace if it weren't for the storms. This thing is just like that. It's black and vicious and deadly, but after it will come the same growth and quickening of life as follow the storm. It will pass."

"Perhaps," Hurst conceded doubtfully. "But it takes a strong faith to see any good coming out of what's going on in this town tonight."

Gradually the screeching turmoil dimmed and subdued. Tired nature was exacting its toll. Along the shadowy streets weary men lurched and staggered in search of rest. The saloons were extinguishing their lights, easing out reluctant die-hards who still persisted in their search for greater hilarity, but were really too tired to put up much of an argument. Horses stood with drooping heads at the hitchracks. Their masters slept in the dust beside them. The kindly dark hid a man who fled in terror for his life. Somewhere a woman screamed like an enraged panther and echoed the scream with shrill, hysterical laughter. A burst of curses was followed by the sodden thud of blows, then silence.

Death lay down the dark side-streets, and

on whiskey-soaked sawdust, and in disordered, deserted tents. Here and there a lurid glow of light hinted at the dissolute license within. The roar of Benton had changed to an incoherent mumble, a feeble yammering that gulped and retched to ghastly stillness.

In the east the sky grayed, blushed rosy red, alchemized to gold. And in the first faint light of the dawn, Benton lay motionless with a semblance of death accentuated by the sprawled forms that lay on disordered beds, in the dust of the street, in corners of darkened rooms. The sun arose in flame and gladness and the rangeland was a beauty that was an exquisite agony to look upon; but Benton lay stark and hideous, exhausted and prostrate. Somewhere a bird sang a note of liquid melody. A lonesome little wind made music in the branches. The waters of the Pecos flashed back the sunlight in spears of silver. The hills stood robed in glory. But Benton slept.

Despite the excitement of the night before, and the lateness of the hour when he went to bed, Walt Slade was awake before mid morning. His left arm was a bit stiff, his cheek a trifle sore, but otherwise he felt fit for anything. After an invigorating sluice in icy water, he headed for the Queen High and breakfast.

He found the saloon freshly scrubbed and shining, with all marks of conflict removed. Algernon Ragnall, the floor manager, was already on the job. His face was the color of a rotten apple, his knuckles gashed and split, but he whistled cheerily as he marshalled his waiters and swampers, who looked as if they didn't like it but figured it best to obey orders.

Slade was just getting ready to eat when John Trout entered and dropped into a chair. He glowered enviously at the tall Ranger.

"Don't know how you do it," he growled as he ordered a cup of black coffee. "My mouth tastes like an old potato and my head is big as a busted accordion and feels in about the same shape, but you look fresh as a daisy."

"Guess I'm copper lined," Slade replied cheerfully as a waiter placed a big plate of ham and eggs before him. Trout turned a little green around the mouth and hastily looked another way.

A few minutes later, Richmond Hurst walked in, his usual handsome, debonair self.

"I'm going to talk with him right now," said Trout. He approached Hurst and the pair entered the back room and shut the door. When they emerged, some time later, both were smiling. Hurst walked to the table and shook hands with Slade.

"Thank you," he said simply. "This is the chance I'd been hoping for. I understand you have agreed to superintend the logging. Doubtless we can arrange adequate compensation."

"Nice of you, but I agreed to handle the chore at the instigation of Mr. Dunn," Slade replied. "He and I will come to terms."

What he didn't tell Hurst was that he was playing a hunch that in some way the activity would provide an opportunity to drop a loop on men who were willing to do murder for gain. He did not believe that Trimble and his associates were ready to admit defeat. Very likely they still had an ace or two up their sleeves.

After a final cup of coffee and a cigarette, Slade sauntered out, leaving Hurst and Trout still discussing business details. He made his way to Deputy Mark Sullivan's little office, where he found Sheriff Dobson alone.

"Well, I've got half a dozen killings to investigate," said the sheriff. "Just a waste of time; nobody will know anything. Happens every payday, but this was the worst of all.

Incidentally, I took a look at that safe door in Trimble's office, as you told me to do. The safe wasn't locked when the charge was fired; the condition of the tumblers and the slots showed that. Do you suppose those two hellions were so stupid as to not try the door before they set off the dynamite?"

"No, they were not stupid," Slade said quietly. Sheriff Dobson shot him a puzzled look.

"Slade," he said plaintively, "won't you tell me a little something of what you know? I'm darned curious, and I might be able to give you a hand, just in case, if I had a notion of what's in the wind."

"Ad," Slade replied, "about the only thing I know for sure is that Parks Trimble is crooked as a snake in a cactus patch. That robbery was staged, just as the fight in the Queen High was staged the night they tried to kill Richmond Hurst. The smaller of those robbers I know was associated with Trimble — they were in the Queen High together last night, Trimble wearing a false beard. They tied Trimble up and gagged him, or pretended to, and then set off the dynamite to make it look good. After they had cleaned the safe and left, Trimble would have shaken the handkerchief off his mouth and started yelling. Sooner or later somebody would have heard him and found him trussed up, with busted sandbags on the floor and the safe presumably blown open, and the money gone. They were careless in the way they handled the dynamite, of course, but the chances are nobody would have noticed, there being no apparent reason for doubting Trimble's account of what happened. Trimble could not have been held accountable for money he placed in the safe as a favor to the saloonkeepers, something, I gather, he had done quite frequently. Just as he never could have been held accountable for the killing of Hurst, if they'd gotten away with it."

"But why would he want Hurst killed?" asked the sheriff.

"Because he had John Trout's note in his possession," Slade explained. "He had put it in his strongbox, with other papers belonging to Hurst, for safe keeping. With Hurst dead, he could have claimed that he bought the note from Hurst, just as Hurst bought it from the bank, and nobody could have refuted the claim. Then with Trout's shipping herd destroyed or his money stolen, as they planned, Trimble would have foreclosed the Lazy K and would have gotten possession of the stand of live oaks on the property that are worth a fortune."

"Live oaks?" repeated the sheriff. Slade explained the business of the trees and their value to the railroad.

"Well, I'll be darned!" exclaimed the sheriff. "Just like John, I never figured those little trees to be worth a hoot. And do you believe the M. K. railroad is mixed up in the deal?"

"Frankly, I don't know," Slade answered. "They may know about those trees, and they may not. But if the M. K. is mixed up in it in some way, in my opinion the M. K. is getting handed a double-cross. They planted Whittaker, the construction engineer, with the C. & P., of course. He built the C. & P. a bridge that would have gone out with the first flash flood that came along. That was to delay the C. & P. and insure the M. K. winning the race to the coast. After he completed the bridge, Whittaker slid out of sight. Perhaps he was associated with Trimble and — somebody else, all the time. Maybe he got in with Trimble later, perhaps through his drinking and gambling. Anyhow, he took part in the raid on Trout's shipping herd and got himself killed. He'd made a survey of the mesa on Trout's land and had the plat in his pocket. I imagine Trimble was depending on him to figure a way to get the trees down from the mesa, which he very likely would have done. They were keeping a close watch on that mesa, perhaps fearing interference of some kind, and that little sidewinder I killed took a shot at Trout and me when we rode up to it. Trigger-happy, I guess, and couldn't resist murdering when he thought he had a chance. Yes, I think the M. K., not particularly noted for ethical practices and not in a position to squawk, was in for a double-cross. If Trimble had gotten possession of the mesa, he would have bid the two roads against each other for the ties and shot the price up. I think whoever bid highest would have gotten them. There's no honor among such an aggregation; it's every man for himself and the devil take the hindmost."

"I've a notion to throw that crooked sidewinder in the calaboose!" growled the sheriff.

"On what charge?" Slade retorted. "For getting robbed? For wearing false whiskers? No law against wearing false whiskers that I know of, unless you could prove they were worn with felonious intent, which you couldn't. No, there's nothing against Trimble that would stand up in court. A good lawyer would make a laughing stock of you. Leave him alone until I give the

193

word. I'm playing a hunch that he'll slip; his sort always does, sooner or later."

"Then you think he's the head of the outfit?"

Slade hesitated before replying. "I'm not sure," he said at length. "Somehow I've a hunch that Trimble just takes orders from a smarter man who is more adept at the double-cross than he is. I haven't much to go on, but I believe it's so. Well, we'll find out. So just take it easy. If I need a hand I'll let you know in a hurry."

"Do that," urged the sheriff. "I don't know how you figure things out like you do; it's beyond me."

"You don't have the advantage of intensive Ranger training," Slade reminded him gently.

"That's so," conceded the sheriff, "but I figure there's a lot more to it than Ranger training."

Slade smiled and didn't argue the point.

"Now I've got to help Trout round up his hands and head back to the ranch," he said. "Things will start moving on that mesa very shortly."

Sixteen

With Jaggers Dunn marshalling all the vast resources of his railroad behind the project, the conveyor system was installed in record time. First a big steam boiler, winding engines and a steam hoist were raised to the cliff crest by means of windlasses manned by muscular arms. Very quickly the steam hoist replaced hand power and all the necessaries for a bunkhouse, storerooms, a kitchen, a barn, and other buildings and equipment were up and set in place. Horses, kicking and plunging in slings, were also sent aloft to draw the logging wagons that would be assembled on the crest of the mesa. The work of felling the trees was ready to begin.

The lumberjacks arrived, tough, brawny men, their foreman a truculent, redhaired giant by the name of Rory Mackay.

Slade led Mackay to the narrow neck of the "hour-glass" and gave him his orders.

"I want the first cutting to go right across here to the far side of the mesa," he explained. "Make it wide, and clear all the underbrush as you go."

"We'd make better time if we cut along the edge of the cliffs first, widening the cutting as we work back," the foreman suggested. "Clearing out all that brush is just a waste of time, too."

Slade glanced toward the costly equipment which had been installed with so much labor, and which would take much precious time to replace, and back to the tinder-dry brush.

"Perhaps," he conceded, "but the way I outlined it is the way I want it done. And, Mackay, I want that cut made as fast as possible."

The foreman shrugged his big shoulders. "You're giving the orders," he said. "I'll do it any way you want it done."

The cutting began. Logs whizzed down the conveyor cables to the plain below, where they were trimmed to shape and hauled to the railroad right-of-way. Slade was pleased with the way things were going, as was John Trout. Richmond Hurst and Verna were frequent visitors to the site of operations, and so was Sheriff Ad Dobson.

Jaggers Dunn sometimes accompanied the

sheriff, for now the railhead was fast approaching Muerto.

"Your ties are sure speeding up things," he told Slade. "Those lumbermen know their business. As fine a bunch of timber as I ever handled."

The lumberjacks had proved to be hard and willing workers, all right. But they also proved to be hard drinkers and spent most of their off hours in the Muerto saloons. In consequence, some were often late for work. After the first week Slade took a hand. He contacted Mackay and his gang in a *cantina,* whooping it up long after midnight.

"Mackay," he quietly told the foreman, "I figure it's time you fellows were in bed."

The big fellow bristled. "Listen, you," he growled, "when we're on the job I take orders from you. When we're not, I don't. Understand?"

Slade nodded. "Just the same, I say it's time you're going back to camp," he replied.

"And maybe you think you can make me go?" Mackay rumbled truculently.

"Yes," Slade said, his voice soft and musical, "I think I can."

Mackay swelled like a turkey gobbler. Then his glance fell to the heavy Colts whose black butts flared out from Slade's muscular thighs.

197

"You wouldn't talk so big if you didn't have those guns hanging on your hips," he sneered.

Slade's slim hands moved with smooth speed. The holstered guns thudded on the bar.

"They're not there now, Mackay," he said with quiet meaning.

The challenge was too direct to be ignored. With a roar of rage, Mackay rushed, huge fists flailing.

Slade stepped lithely forward to meet him. His left hand lashed out. Mackay rose from his feet, shot through the air and hit the floor with a crash that shook the building. He bounded to his feet like a rubber ball, blood spewing from his cut lips, and rushed again. Slade met him with hard lefts and rights that rocked his head. Mackay bored in, caught Slade on the jaw with a slashing right that almost knocked the Ranger off balance. He lunged back and they met shoulder to shoulder, slugging it out, while the lumberjacks, hopping with excitement, cheered both impartially. Both men were bleeding now, and breathing hard. Slade rocked Mackay's head with a straight right to the jaw, took a left hook in return, countered with an uppercut to the jaw and brought grunts from his opponent with a drive to the midriff, and danced away. Mackay staggered back, lowered his red head and hurled himself at his elusive adversary. Slade hit him twice but couldn't stop him. The giant ducked under another blow, closed, and wrapped his great arms about the Ranger's middle. Mightily he wrestled, striving to sweep Slade off his feet.

"Rory's got the under-holt — that feller's a goner!" yelped a lumberjack.

But he wasn't. As Mackay strained and grunted, a corded arm shoved under his chin. Its mate clamped across his forehead. Great muscles showed plainly through Slade's shirt as he put forth his strength.

Slowly, slowly the big fellow's head was forced back and up, until the strain on the cervical spine was more than he could bear. He loosed his hold and staggered back.

Slade hit him, hard and true, on the angle of the jaw. Rory Mackay whirled, sagged, crashed to the floor and lay with arms widespread, his bloody face buried in the sawdust.

But as Slade knelt beside him, a bit anxiously, he groaned, twitched, rolled over on his back and with Slade's assistance sat up, staring dazedly. Then, as his head cleared, his bloody lips split in a grin. He leaped lightly to his feet and stretched out a big paw.

"Slade," he said, "you're a good man, a raunchin' good man! I'd like to feel the grip of your hand!"

Solemnly they shook hands, while the lumberjacks whooped and cheered and slapped their thighs with calloused palms.

As their hands fell apart, Rory Mackay turned to his grinning men.

"Boys," he said, "Mr. Slade said it was time for us fellers to hit the hay. I reckon it is!"

After Slade's disciplining of Rory Mackay, with whom he quickly established a warm friendship, things went along smoothly for some days. Too smoothly, Slade thought. He suffered an uneasy presentiment that something was due to happen.

It was, and it did. First the Pecos weather gods, always a dour and unpredictable lot, decided to take a hand. One afternoon a great purple cloud rolled up from the southeast, heavy and piled. Slowly it climbed the long blue slant of the heavens. The sun was snuffed out like a candle dip and dark shadows swept across the land. The air was hot and oppressive, but oddly chilly at times. Slade knew the barometer reading must be very low and wished he had an instrument to check.

On and on rolled the purple cloud, until the whole sky was covered and all things were shrouded in an unholy yellow twilight. Above was the leaden, flattened arch that seemed to press down on the cowering earth, below the eerie shadows. Glancing up, Slade saw flocks of birds flying northward, but the usual calling amid the trees was stilled. He shook his head. The feathered songsters knew there was trouble in the making and were getting in the clear.

"If we were farther east, I'd say a Gulf hurricane was headed this way," he observed to Rory Mackay. "As it is, I'm afraid we're in for a bad blow, and we're rather exposed up here."

"I've a notion the trees will break most of the wind," replied the foreman. "They won't suffer, either; they're too small and sturdy. We'll make out."

"I hope so," Slade replied. "You'd better call the boys in and batten down everything that's loose. I'm going below to stable my horse and see that things are ship-shape down there. Be back in a little while.

Slade had caused a small shelter to be built at the base of the cliffs and a little to the north of the hoist, where Shadow, who was usually turned loose on the prairie, could take refuge during inclement weather. He made sure the big horse was snug, inspected the equipment and returned to the mesa top, where he found everything possible had been done to safeguard the camp.

The dark closed down, pitch-black. The night was deathly still, with no leaf moving, not a breath of air stirring. All nature seemed big with impending disaster. The sky appeared to be sinking down on the earth. The stars were hidden, of course, yet a faint and lurid light shone now in one quarter of the horizon, now in another. Doubtless the reflection of distant lightning. Despite the lack of wind, the air seemed to moan audibly.

"Acts like the end of the world was near," chuckled Rory Mackay.

"Probably may be the case, so far as we are concerned, if what's coming is bad as it looks to be," Slade replied grimly.

The hours dragged on, with always the same black dark, always the same unearthly stillness, against which the small sounds of the camp beat loudly and echoed back. Finally all activity died down and the men congregated in the big bunkhouse to smoke and talk, for nobody had any intention of going to bed.

Midnight came and went. Another hour passed slowly. Then Slade, who was sitting by an open window, heard a faint sighing, like to the susurrus of the incoming tide. From the southeast it came, swelling to a whisper, a murmur, a low mutter. He stood up and closed the window.

"It's coming," he said.

Louder and louder grew the ominous sound, and overhead thunder grumbled. The tree leaves were rustling now, the branches groaning.

With the bellow of an aroused giant the storm struck. A mighty blast of wind rocked the bunkhouse. Another and another. Then a sustained pressure of displaced air like to flowing water. The gale howled and shrieked, growing stronger by the second. And on the wings of that screaming wind came rain and huge hail stones that beat on the roof with a perpetual rattling roar, that in its sum Slade thought was one of the most terrible sounds to which he ever listened. He began to fear that the roof would be battered in, or that the walls would crumble beneath this incessant fire of the musketry of heaven.

And through the infernal uproar faintly threaded another and even more terrible sound, the screaming of terrified horses.

Slade reached for his slicker, donned it and buttoned it tight. He jammed his hat down on his head.

"What the devil you going to do?" demanded Mackay. "You aren't going out in that?"

"Got to," Slade answered. "I'm heading for the barn. If those horses aren't quieted they'll break loose and kick each other to death. They're going loco."

"I'm coming along," said Mackay, reaching for his own slicker. Slade waited until he had donned it, then opened the door. A blast of wind and rain set the lamps to smoking. Hail stones hopped about the floor like living things. Slade banged the door shut and they were exposed to the full fury of the storm. Lightning blazed, thunder rolled. The wind tore at them. The hail struck them stinging blows. Suddenly there was a rending and splintering. The lightning flared and showed something huge and dark that rushed through the air and hit the ground with a crash. It was the roof of the cook shanty.

"Feller, I'm scairt!" shouted Mackay. "If that thing had come this way, we'd have never knowed what hit us!"

"Maybe there won't be any more," Slade shouted back. "Come on!"

Heads down, they battled their way to the barn, which was a bedlam of neighings and stampings, flung open the door and closed it again with difficulty. While Slade soothed the frightened animals with voice and hand, Mackay found a lantern and lighted it. The horses, reassured by human companionship, quieted down. Slade doffed his streaming slicker, fished the makin's from his shirt pocket and rolled cigarettes. Seated with their backs to the wall, they smoked leisurely. The barn shook and quivered to the blasts of the wind, and the rain and hail hammered the roof, but it was sturdily built and Slade did not think it would collapse.

An hour passed, and the storm showed signs of abating. After a while they heard shouts outside. They opened the door and saw lanterns bobbing about through the rain, which had subsided to a drizzle. The wind had lost much of its strength. The ground appeared buried beneath a veil of snow, but as the normal temperature reasserted itself, the skim of hail melted rapidly.

Approaching the unroofed cook shanty, Slade found the old cook dancing about in front of his ruined headquarters as vigorously as though he had just been bitten by a scorpion.

"All the flour sp'ilt! All the coffee sp'ilt!" he howled. "Everything the dad-blasted rain could hurt is sp'ilt! What the devil are we going to eat, I'd like to know!"

"Take it easy," Slade told him. "It'll be light in another hour and I'll ride to town and order fresh supplies sent out pronto."

The rain ceased to fall. The wind died to a whisper. Slade made sure the machinery had suffered no serious damage and called the hoist engineer.

"You can send me down, now," he said. "I'll get my horse and head for Muerto."

Reaching the ground below, Slade made his way to Shadow's little stable and opened the door. The big black welcomed him with a snort but showed no signs of having been particularly perturbed by the recent uproar. Slade put a helping of oats in his manger and smoked while Shadow ate his fill, which took some time. When he was sure the horse's hunger was assuaged, he gave him a drink and cinched the saddle into place. Opening the door, he stepped out to find that the east was already graying. He glanced toward the hoist and saw a form run swiftly from the framework and disappear in the shadows. At the base of the hoist was a sputtering of reddish sparks, a crawling flower of fire.

Slade bounded forward, dived between the supporting timbers. Lying against one was a bundle of dynamite sticks, capped and fused. He seized the fizzing sheaf of death, saw that there was no time to cut the fuse; the fire was lapping the cap. Drawing back his arm, he hurled the lethal bundle far out onto the prairie, and threw himself to the ground.

The dynamite exploded in mid-air with a deafening roar and a blinding flash of yellow light. The concussion was terrific. It lifted Slade from the ground, slammed him down again. The report reverberated from the cliffs. The massive timbers of the hoist creaked and groaned. Slade lay gasping for a moment, then scrambled to his feet.

From the shadows at the cliff base fire spurted. Slade whirled about and pitched headlong.

SEVENTEEN

Half stunned by the blow of the slug that had grazed his temple, Slade dimly heard, through the bell notes storming in his ears, the beat of fast hoofs fading into the distance. With a mighty effort of the will, he summoned enough strength to lurch erect, shaking his head to free it of the fog that shrouded his brain. In the growing light, he saw a horseman some hundred yards to the south, going like the wind.

Slade whistled a clear note. Shadow trotted from the stable, saddle leather popping. Slade had some difficulty forking him, but he managed it. His voice rang out —

"Trail, feller, trail!"

Shadow shot forward. The rush of cool air quickly cleared Slade's mind. He settled his feet firmly in the stirrups, loosened his Winchester in its sheath. The fugitive was mounted on a tall bay that was going strong, but Slade was confident that Shadow's great speed and endurance would quickly close the gap. He began counting off the shrinking distance — a thousand yards — nine-fifty — nine hundred. The bay was giving his all, but it was not enough. Eight hundred — seven hundred — six-fifty!

"Just a little more, feller," he told Shadow. "Just a little more and maybe we can persuade that gent to pull up, before he stops for good. If we can take him alive we may learn a few things from him. Just a little more! Confound that bulge!"

Directly ahead of the speeding bay the cliff jutted outward. He swerved around the bulge and disappeared from Slade's sight.

Slade slackened speed a little as he neared the bulge, although he did not believe the fellow would stop to shoot it out with him. Watchful and alert, his rifle ready for instant action, he rounded the jut of cliff — and stared incredulously.

Ahead the prairie stretched empty; there was no sign of the fugitive. Slade's gaze shifted to the cliff. They were absolutely sheer, an unbroken wall of stone. On the rocky slopes leading up to them were certainly no boulders large enough to hide a horse.

A mile farther on was a second bulge, but it seemed inconceivable that the bay could

209

have covered the distance in so short a period of time. But where else had he gotten to? Slade sent Shadow surging forward. He circled away from the cliffs, for if the hellion was holed up some place or had conveniently become invisible, he might announce his presence with a shot. But Slade's keen gaze could discern no possible concealment. He quickened Shadow's pace even more.

They careened around the second bulge. Slade pulled up. Again the prairie stretched untenanted before him. And still the cliffs were sheer.

Farther to the south, however, were thickets. If his quarry had taken refuge in one of those, to approach them over the open prairie would just be a nice way of committing suicide. He might as well face it — somehow he had been neatly outsmarted.

After studying the distances ahead for some time, he turned Shadow and headed back north, again circling away from the cliffs, again eyeing them with searching gaze. Finally he shook his head in disgust.

"Seems I'm developing a perfect genius for doing stupid things," he grumbled to the horse. "I should have known that devil would wait in the dark to see what happened, and throw lead at me if he got a

210

chance. But after the explosion, I hopped right up off the ground to give him a fair mark. Only bull luck and poor shooting on his part saved me. Close as the devil as it was," he added, gingerly probing the bullet burn alongside his temple with a forefinger. "Well, as I've said before, live and learn! That is, if you can manage to live long enough.' "

At the foot of the hoist, Slade found Rory Mackay and several others awaiting him.

"What the devil happened?" demanded the foreman. "Sounded like the world had busted."

Slade told him. Mackay shook his red head and swore. "Figured to blow up the hoist, eh?"

"Yes," Slade replied. "It would have taken us days to clean up the mess and rebuild the darn thing. The cutting would have been delayed and the railroad held up for want of ties. A nice try, all right, and likely there'll be others, seeing as this one didn't work. But I'd sure like to know how that hellion gave me the slip."

"And I'd sure like to get my hands on him," growled Mackay opening and shutting his huge paws. "I'd take him apart and scatter him all the way from here to Muerto! Now what?"

"Now I'm heading for town and those supplies," Slade said, gathering up the reins.

"Think it's safe?"

"I think it's highly unlikely that the sidewinder would hole up and wait for me to come back, once he's in the clear," Slade answered. "I'll be seeing you."

Slade rode warily, again circling the cliffs, and again studying them intently, with barren results. He reached town without incident and after making sure the needed supplies were on the move, rode back to the camp, where he found the damage wrought by the storm was being repaired.

"I like this job," chuckled Mackay. "Always something going on, and always a chance to get into a fight."

Slade was continually prowling about the plateau, keeping an eye on things in general and a close watch for anything out of the ordinary, for he was still far from assured that Parks Trimble and his bunch would not make any further move. In fact, he thought it highly likely that they would, and endeavored to anticipate and guard against whatever turn their devilish ingenuity might take. And he was still playing the hunch that in some connection with the logging venture, Trimble and his associates would tip their hand and give him the opportunity he hoped for.

One morning he was sauntering south across the mesa a mile or so below the camp when a plaintive whinney sounded nearby. Glancing about, he spotted a horse peering from a nearby thicket. A broken bridle dangled from the rusty bit in its sore mouth and its sides showed the marks of a saddle recently rubbed off against tree trunks or by vigorous rolling.

"Now where in blazes did you come from?" he asked. He approached the animal, which made no move to run away, and removed the hit from its mouth. He stroked its neck, rubbed its nose and smoothed out its tangled mane.

"I'll take you to camp with me for a helping of oats and a currying and brushing," he promised, "but I sure wish you'd tell me how you got here. That little drygulcher I shot off the bluff must have ridden you up, but where?"

The horse, while undoubtedly appreciating his ministrations, did not answer, which was not particularly surprising. Freed of the hampering bit, it began to graze contentedly. Slade gazed at it, his brows drawing together. "So there *is* a way up here," he mused. From his pocket he drew the survey

213

of the mesa and studied it, tracing the wavering line marked "possible" with his finger. He estimated that the spot shouldn't be more than a mile to the south, if the plat was accurate, and he had no reason to believe it was not. He replaced the paper and headed south.

He had covered something less than a mile when he came to a peculiar formation, the first of its kind he had noted on the mesa.

Scoring the plateau from east to west was a wide, dry wash where no trees or brush grew. It had doubtless been scoured out in the course of the years by melting snow and heavy rain. There was a slight slope toward it from both north and south. Slade followed the depression toward the western cliffs. As it neared the cliffs, it turned sharply south, running parallel to the naked wall of stone that hemmed it on the west. For more than a mile the southerly trend continued, then once more it veered west, steadily deepening until it became a narrow crevice scoring downward through the cliff face at a steep angle. Not too steep, however, for a horse to negotiate.

Slade continued through deepening gloom. After a bit the cleft of the wash again abruptly slanted to the south, until it almost paralleled the face of the cliff. The light began to strengthen and a few minutes later he stepped onto the rock slope at the base of the mesa. As he did so, he noted that the angle of the crevice was such that the opening would not be discernible to anyone riding the plain beyond the shallow slope.

So that was how the devil who tried to dynamite the hoist gave him the slip! Slid into this crack and holed up snug till his pursuer gave up the chase. Chances are he was laughing his head off as Slade rode up and down the prairie like he was trying to catch moonbeams. The thought did not improve El Halcon's temper.

Banishing his anger as just an additional show of stupidity, Slade ran his eye over the rock strewn descent to the level rangeland.

Yes, it would be possible to build a logging road down the wash and across the slope. However, the conveyor system was much better, and cheaper in the long run. But the unexpected route of descent from the crest was a good thing to remember, and not talk about, he concluded. The drygulcher who took the shot at him and John Trout had made his way to the summit via this route. Which meant that the whole bunch, including Trimble, must know about it. He reclimbed the cleft and followed the wash to the east cliffs, where it proved too

215

precipitous for even a man on foot to descend. He picked up the horse on his way back and placed it in the barn without mentioning to anybody the incident of its discovery.

Slade fully intended to post a guard at the upper opening of the cleft, just in case somebody might take a notion to come snooping around, but after all he was only human. When he got back to the camp, Rory Mackay was waiting for him with a number of problems that demanded his immediate attention, and the matter of posting the guard slipped his mind. From that neglect came trouble.

Once again everything was progressing smoothly. Once again too darn smoothly, Slade felt. The unnatural quiet was a bit ominous, something in the nature of the calm before the storm, hinting at a gathering of forces for an attack. For Slade was convinced that Trimble and his bunch, very probably with M. K. backing, were just awaiting an opportunity to strike where it would hurt most. Well, that could well give him the opportunity he hoped for — the opportunity to drop a loop on the lawbreakers. Which, after all, was the real reason for him being in the section.

But as the days passed peacefully, he

began to experience a certain disquietude. Looked like his hunch was not going to work out. And Captain McNelty didn't send him here to fell trees or build railroad, but to apprehend certain trouble makers. Slade felt that he was falling down on the job.

There was another matter that gave him concern. Because of the luxuriance of the tree growth, the cutting across the neck of the mesa proceeded slowly. Slade insisted that all brush be cleared away, all tops hauled some distance to the north. He breathed easier when he estimated that they had less than a quarter of a mile to go to reach the eastern cliffs. He felt that the camp and its costly equipment were now fairly safe, but he was bothered about the trees. It was late autumn and the sap was sluggish, the leaves blazing with color and getting dryer every day. The undergrowth was like tinder and grew heavily between the trunks, especially to the north, where by far the greater portion of the trees stood.

John Trout was in a jubilant mood. "I feel like I'm settin' on top of the world," he confided to Slade, "and it's all due to you. Hurst has sold his saloon to Ragnall, his floor manager, on easy terms. Ragnall figures there'll be enough business in Benton, with its shipping pens and shops to keep the place going."

"He's right," Slade agreed. "Algy is well liked and will draw plenty of trade."

"And Hurst has had several offers for his new place in Muerto now that everybody knows Muerto is going to the Division," Trout continued. "He's going to let that go, too, and buy a slice in the Lazy K."

"Fine!" Slade applauded. "I think he'll be happier raising cows than selling whiskey. And that will keep Verna close to you," he added with a smile.

"Which helps," Trout nodded. "An old man gets sort of lonely by himself, especially when the sun goes down." He glanced a bit wistfully at the tall Ranger. "Wish you could see your way to stick around, too, son," he said, "but I guess you won't. A rambler's a rambler, and there ain't no cure for that disease but going places."

"Anyhow, I'll be back to see you, that I promise," Slade said, his cold eyes abruptly all kindness.

Yes, things were going smoothly, the operation proceeding like clockwork. And then what promised to be disaster struck. The morning had dawned clear, with the prevailing wind blowing from the southeast and steadily strengthening. Slade, after bringing Shadow to the crest, via the hoist, had ridden to the east end of the cutting where Rory Mackay and his men were busily at work. Suddenly the big foreman raised his red head and sniffed sharply.

"Don't I be smelling wood smoke?" he said.

Slade also smelled it. His gaze raised to the tree tops, traveled south and centered on a dark stain fouling the clear blue of the sky.

"You do," he said, his voice sharp and brittle. "Rory, it's a brush fire down there to the south, and close. This side of the big dry wash. I've been afraid something like this might happen. Now you see why I insisted this cutting be made straight across the mesa and all the underbrush cleared away. We've got our work cut out for us. Clear the brush to the cliffs as fast as you can. Never mind the trees — they won't catch if the brush is cleared away; there's still some sap in the trunks and branches, but not enough to resist the burning brush. Start a backfire to the south as you go. I'll grab everybody left at the camp and start one from that end. Move!"

With a roar, Mackay leaped into action. He and his men had fought forest fires before and knew exactly what was to be done. Axes flashed, brawny arms strained.

219

The smoke from the backfire set to meet the flames roaring up from the south rose against the sky, whipped into fantastic shapes by the howling wind.

Slade sent Shadow racing westward. Everybody at the camp was out already. They, too, were experienced hands from cooks and wranglers to laborers and stable boys. They had a backfire going and were feeding it eastward as fast as possible. Slade rode back to the scene of the cutting, where the danger was greatest. The smoke was rolling from the south in clouds. Brands and hot ash were falling; but the cutting was broad and save for a fitful flare now and then did no harm.

It was different where the brush still grew. The conflagration was racing toward it at frightful speed.

Faster and faster flew the axes. The brush was felled and dragged away. Slade superintended the setting of the backfire, which he kept as close on the heels of the loggers as he dared. A little miscalculation and the kindled flames would get out of control and be but an ally to the main holocaust thundering up from the south.

Rory Mackay paused to wipe his grimy face. He grinned at Slade through the smoke. "It's going to be touch-and-go, but we'll make it," he declared and bent to swing his big axe the faster.

Now the air quivered to an ominous roaring. Time and again the lofty crown of one of the forest giants burst into flame to burn a fiery torch against the swirling smoke. Beneath was a seething caldron of destruction racing north on the wings of the wind.

"Think we'll lose the trees to the south?" panted Mackay.

"No, it'll never jump that wide dry wash against the wind," Slade replied. "Thank the Lord that thing runs clean across the mesa. No, our danger lies here."

Through smoke and burning ash and flame they fought their way to the cliffs, the backfire burning sluggishly against the beat of the wind but fast enough to clear a space of sufficient width where there remained no fuel to feed the ravening monster that threatened the mesa with destruction. Slade swung an axe in the forefront, Rory Mackay another. Finally the Ranger paused on the very edge of the cliff. Shadow, who had paced behind his master all the way, blew prodigiously, sneezed and snorted with disgust.

"That does it," Slade said. "And a job to be proud of. I'll see to it that you fellows have a bust in town to remember."

The smoky loggers croaked a cheer, grinning like so many end men at a minstrel show. Slade walked to Shadow and tightened the cinches.

"Got a little chore to do," he told Mackay. "Do I think the fire was deliberately set? I do."

Another moment and he was gone, racing Shadow through the still drifting smoke, leaving the big foreman cursing behind him.

When he reached the camp, Slade sent Shadow straight for the hoist, which was barely large enough to accommodate the tall black.

"Send us down in a hurry," he told the engineer at the control.

The descent was made at a speed that took the breath away. At the base of the cliff Slade found a crowd assembled, among them Sheriff Ad Dobson.

"We saw the smoke from town and figured we'd better hustle up here and see what was happening," the sheriff said.

"Glad you're here," Slade said tersely. "Come on, I think it's showdown." He turned Shadow's head to the south.

"Where are we going and what are we going to do?" Dobson asked as he reined in alongside the Ranger.

"A snake usually comes out by way of the

222

hole he goes in," Slade replied. "If we sift sand I believe we can drop a loop on the sidewinders. That fire was deliberately set, Ad, and I'm banking on the firebugs to hang around on top of the mesa for a while to see how successful they were. They wouldn't be able to tell right away whether we managed to get the fire under control. I don't think they have any idea that I know about their private back door, a wash that provides a path up the cliff that can be negotiated by horses."

"Do you figure it's Trimble?" asked the sheriff.

"Yes, and perhaps the real he-wolf of the pack is with him," Slade answered. "I hope so, for I've a notion the only way to get anything on that clever homed toad is to catch him in the act. Be ready for business. Any talking that's done will very likely be through the smoke. I don't think they'll give up unless they see the case is hopeless, and that sort seldom considers it hopeless so long as they can pull trigger. Be ready, and watch out for some unexpected trick. They're smart as a tree full of owls."

"I'll make 'em smart if they try something," growled the sheriff. "I've got a score to settle with that bunch; they've made me look as awkward as a little black fellow with a big navel." Slade chuckled and urged Shadow to greater speed.

They reached the point where the dry wash opened through the face of the cliff. Slade turned onto the slope, loosening his Winchester in the scabbard. They threaded their way up the rock strewn rise to the base of the cliff.

But the gloomy mouth of the slanting cleft was devoid of sound or motion when they reached it. Slade dismounted, motioning the sheriff to do likewise. They led their horses a little to one side, left them standing and took up stations facing the cleft.

A tense and tedious half hour passed. Slade began to wonder if the quarry had left the mesa immediately after setting the fire. Another ten minutes were likewise barren of results.

Then sound trickled from the crevice mouth, steadily growing louder. It resolved to the clashing of horses' irons on the stone. Another moment and three men rode out of the crevice, conversing animatedly. One, a hulking individual with a blocky face, Slade instantly recognized as the fellow who tried to knife Richmond Hurst in the course of the fight in the Queen High. On his left rode Parks Trimble. On his right Jason Gaunt, the new manager of the Muerto bank. So engrossed were the trio in their discussion that they did not see the grim figures standing in the shadow of the cliff until Slade's voice rang out —

"In the name of the State of Texas! You are under arrest! Elevate!"

Heads jerked to the front; the horses halted. The three stared in paralyzed amazement. Their hands slowly rose, until they were shoulder high. Slade took a half step forward.

Jason Gaunt's slender right hand shot forward like the head of a striking snake. A stubby little double-barrelled derringer spatted into his palm from his sleeve — the gambler's draw — and spurted fire.

But even as he pressed trigger he whirled sideways from his horse, his breast riven and shattered by the slugs from the Ranger's guns.

Sheriff Dobson was shooting with both hands, answering the fire of the owlhoots, who had flashed into action with their leader's move. Slade's Colts joined in a drumroll of thundering reports.

In five seconds it was all over. Slade lowered his smoking guns and gazed at the three figures on the ground. Gaunt alone still showed signs of life.

Slade holstered his guns, strode forward

and knelt beside the dying man. Gaunt's glazing eyes glared up at him with bitter hate.

"Blast you, so you're taking over!" he frothed through his bloody lips.

Slade slowly shook his head. From a cunningly concealed secret pocket in his broad leather belt he drew the famous silver star set on a silver circle, the feared and honored badge of the Texas Rangers.

"Yes, I'm taking over, Gaunt, but not the way you think," he said as he held the gleaming star before the bank manager's fixed eyes.

"A Ranger!" Gaunt gasped. "El Halcon a Texas Ranger!"

"Yes," Slade replied.

Gaunt strove to speak again but choked on the blood welling in his throat, and choking, died. Slade stood up and slipped the silver star back in its pocket.

"I guess that's about all," he said to the sheriff, in a tired voice.

Dobson was staring at the dead Gaunt, on his face an expression of utter bewilderment.

"Gaunt!" he sputtered. "The bank manager! Well, I'll be hanged!"

"I suspected him of something off-color the first time I saw him," Slade said.

"Why?" asked the sheriff.

"Because of his hands."

"His hands?"

"Yes," Slade replied. "He had gambler's hands, beautifully cared for, the nails filed to tiny sharp points, the tips of the fingers showing signs of having been sandpapered. And when he hammered the desk with his fist, to drive home a point to John Trout, I distinctly heard the thud of metal and knew he had a gun in a sleeve holster, a sure mark of the professional gambler. A queer get-up for a bank official. Then I saw him associating with Parks Trimble and knew I was right. In my opinion Gaunt was a trouble shooter for the M. K., hired to direct such jobs as the bridge and this one of firing the mesa. Sometimes businessmen who are honest, according to their own lights, hire such characters to take care of off-color chores. Chisum and Murphy did it in the row between the big ranchers and the small cattlemen when they hired Billy the Kid, Doc Skurlock and Bowdrie and others of like kidney to do their fighting for them. Of course, the hellions got out of hand; the result, the Lincoln County War, with killings a-plenty."

Dobson shook his head but did not otherwise comment. Slade continued:

227

"But as I told you once before, I'm pretty sure the M. K. was all set to be handed a doublecross. When that didn't work out, Gaunt and Trimble turned back to their chore of delaying the C. & P. as much as possible. The M. K. got a bad jolt when the C. & P. acquired the ties and other timber it needed right here in the section. If the trees had been destroyed, the M. K. would have been back in the running. We have nothing on the M. K., of course, but Captain McNelty will have a little talk with those gentlemen and, I don't doubt, make them see the error of their ways. Well, we might as well rope the carcasses to the horses and head back to the camp. We've done all we can here. You can explain things to folks in Muerto."

When they arrived below the site of the camp with their grim burdens, they found John Trout and others awaiting them. Slade let Sheriff Dobson do the explaining, which the sheriff did ably enough. Slade got the rig off Shadow and turned him loose to graze.

"And now," he suggested, "suppose we go up top and have a snack and a cup of coffee. I feel I can use both; and a good wash won't hurt, either."

When they had finished eating, Slade

stepped out of the cook shanty and glanced at the sun. The camp was still smoky and powdered with black ash, but the fire had burned down to angry sputterings.

"Well, it looks like everything is under control here," he observed. "It isn't late, so I think I'll take me a ride. I want to have a little talk with Mr. Dunn, whom I understand is in Benton. John, I'll stop at the ranchhouse and say goodbye to Verna before I hit the Pecos Trail."

They watched him ride away, tall and graceful atop his great black horse, the low-lying sun etching his sternly handsome profile in flame, to where duty called and danger and new adventure waited.

"And there goes the notorious El Halcon, riding off again after shooting a lot of folks," chuckled Sheriff Dobson.

"Ad," said old John, "I don't know what he is, but the way he handles men and takes care of rascals, I know what he ought to be."

"What?" asked the sheriff, his eyes twinkling.

"A Texas Ranger!"

229

ABOUT THE AUTHOR

Bradford Scott was a pseudonym for **Leslie Scott** who was born in Lewisburg, West Virginia. During the Great War, he joined the French Foreign Legion and spent four years in the trenches. In the 1920s he worked as a mining engineer and bridge builder in the western American states and in China before settling in New York. A barroom discussion in 1934 with Leo Margulies, who was managing editor for Standard Magazines, prompted Scott to try writing fiction. He went on to create two of the most notable series characters in Western pulp magazines. In 1936, Standard Magazines launched, and in *Texas Rangers,* Scott under the house name of **Jackson Cole** created Jim Hatfield, Texas Ranger, a character whose popularity was so great with readers that this magazine featuring his adventures lasted until 1958. When others eventually began contributing Jim Hatfield stories,

Scott created another Texas Ranger hero, Walt Slade, better known as *El Halcon,* the Hawk, whose exploits were regularly featured in *Thrilling Western.* In the 1950s Scott moved quickly into writing book-length adventures about both Jim Hatfield and Walt Slade in long series of original paperback Westerns. At the same time, however, Scott was also doing some of his best work in hardcover Westerns published by Arcadia House; thoughtful, well-constructed stories, with engaging characters and authentic settings and situations. Among the best of these, surely, are *Silver City* (1953), *Longhorn Empire* (1954), *The Trail Builders* (1956), and *Blood on the Rio Grande* (1959). In these hardcover Westerns, many of which have never been reprinted, Scott proved himself highly capable of writing traditional Western stories with characters who have sufficient depth to change in the course of the narrative and with a degree of authenticity and historical accuracy absent from many of his series stories.

We hope you have enjoyed this Large Print book. Other Thorndike, Wheeler, and Chivers Press Large Print books are available at your library or directly from the publishers.

For information about current and upcoming titles, please call or write, without obligation, to:

Publisher
Thorndike Press
295 Kennedy Memorial Drive
Waterville, ME 04901
Tel. (800) 223-1244

or visit our Web site at:

http://gale.cengage.com/thorndike

OR

Chivers Large Print
published by BBC Audiobooks Ltd
St James House, The Square
Lower Bristol Road
Bath BA2 3SB
England
Tel. +44(0) 800 136919
email: bbcaudiobooks@bbc.co.uk
www.bbcaudiobooks.co.uk

All our Large Print titles are designed for easy reading, and all our books are made to last.